Zera has grown up on a world where actives develop superpowers and are less than fifteen percent of the population. It is expected that actives serve society, but some of them have other ideas.

Zera is a master of weapons design, but her active nature is that of a hopper. She can literally jump into someone else's body and hide inside. Her sister, Susara, is Suit Bait. She projects vulnerability, which attracts the right and wrong type of interest.

When Susara's soul is shattered and she is left to die, Zera sets a series of actions in motion that involve a superhero escort service, patrons who pay extensively for the pleasure of a superhuman partner, and clients with very specific needs.

The Blind Date Corporation arranges dates between patrons and the escorts, while the escorts wear a mask that covers their eyes and blurs the memories of the patrons so that no stalker issues arise. The company is flourishing until one of the original patrons from the days before the masks outs Zera as an escort, and the entire plan of revenge for Susa's death ramps up a notch. Super.

The characters and events in this book are fictitious. Any similarity to real persons, living or dead, is coincidental and not intended by the author.

I Dated a Supervillain
Copyright © 2021 by Viola Grace
ISBN: 978-1-989892-79-4

©Cover art by Angela Waters

Published by Viola Grace

Look for me online at violagrace.com.

# I Dated a Supervillain
## Blind Date Corporation Book 1

## By

## Viola Grace

# Chapter One

Zera got up at five, got dressed, and prepared to go running, just like she did every morning. She knocked on Susara's bedroom door and paused when it swung open. Her message unit was blinking.

Zera walked over to the unit and pressed the activator.

Susara's voice came to her, slurring and giggling. "Zera, today's the day. Delvis said he was going to tell the boss that we are in love."

"Oh, Susa. No." Zera lifted her arm and activate the tracker. She started running while the message continued.

She sprinted out of their small house, down the sidewalk, and got onto her rider. She pulled the helmet on and keyed up emergency services to meet her at the tracking point. She would take the fines if she was wrong. She hoped she was fucking wrong.

The streets were nearly empty, and she passed slow-moving traffic as she headed toward the waterfront. Tears were tracking down her face as she pulled up to the obelisk where Susara's limp body was lying.

"Nonononononono." She dumped her bike and ran to Susara. She was in her prettiest dress and limp in Zera's arms as she was lifted onto her lap. Her eyes were wide open, and there was no consciousness inside. Zera closed her eyes and rocked the living body that had been purged of its soul. Susa was dead.

Emergency services pulled up, and Zera looked at the peacekeepers who approached her with weapons drawn. With her helmet and exercise gear, she looked like a super. She released Susa carefully and lay on her stomach, letting

1

them subdue her so they could help her friend.

It took a few minutes before they remembered to scan her identity, and when they did, the cuffs came off.

"I need to head to the hospital that they are taking her to." Zera watched them lifting Susa into an ambulance.

The peacekeeper helped her up. "Does she have any next of kin?"

"No. She's in the program, and her parents are dead. I am her medical proxy and her executor."

"How did you know she was here?" An investigator walked up and looked her over. His eyes lingered on her curves, and she gave him a bland look.

"She is in the program and is chipped. She wasn't in her room, and she left me a message." She looked toward the ambulance. "She was going to tell the guy she was dating that she was in love with someone else."

"You think he did this?"

She looked at the vehicle as it drove off. "I know he did."

"How do you know that?"

"Because she was—oh, there they are. Sorry. This is now out of your paygrade."

A slick vehicle comprised of the highest-level experimental tech pulled up. She should know; she designed it. The team that spilled out came directly toward her. She looked at them and pulled her helmet off.

The three heroes in armoured suits nodded to her. One said, "Madame Zera, we came when we got the message."

"I need my home secured, a full investigation begun, and a notice of her coma sent to the program directors. I am going to do everything in my power to get her to the trials in a week, but to do that, I need to get to the hospital."

Astel nodded. "I will take you to the hospital."

Naima smiled politely. "I will take your cycle and helmet, Researcher."

Hron inclined his head. "I will drive the vehicle and get all recordings from this area to find out who dumped her here."

Zera nodded. "Please, forward me what you find."

Hron nodded. "Of course."

Astel picked her up, and he murmured, "Cover your ears."

She settled against him and covered her ears. He launched skyward and took them past the ambulance, landing at the hospital.

"We're here."

She nodded and made sure that her hands were shaking nervously as he set her on her feet. "Thanks, Astel."

"No problem. This is horrible. Susara was ... is amazing."

"Even though most considered her Suit Bait?" Zera looked at him, and he turned his head away.

"About that. I didn't actually mean it; everyone was saying it."

"Not everyone. Just a bunch of guys with very small dicks and girls with flat chests. She was genetically gifted, just like the team applicants; she just had much better fashion sense."

She was tapping on her com while she spoke, and in the three minutes that it took for the ambulance to arrive, the program had sent a collection vehicle.

Zera stopped the doctors at the hospital and transferred Susa to the dark vehicle the program had sent via the loading dock. One look at her credentials was enough to get the folk at the hospital to step back.

She entered their computer and created a fictional patient entry, pulling in scans from the ambulance and making the room Susa was supposedly in a janitor's closet. Just in case someone tried to come in and finish what the mind-wiper had started. Once she had set things in motion, she headed down to the hire car bay and got a vehicle to take her home. Astel would figure things out, or he wouldn't.

Hron called on her com. *"What did you do with Astel?"*

"Nothing. He gave me a lift to the hospital, and I had some administration to attend to. I have no idea where he is." She sighed. "I am heading home to get a download of Susara's files. I have to redact any information that involves my research projects."

*"Oh. Of course. Will we get a copy of that?"*

"It will be provided to the teams. Yes. I should be done with it this afternoon."

Hron's voice was concerned. *"How are you holding up?"*

"Fairly well. We planned for this. There are contingencies in place."

*"You planned for Susa to die?"*

"No. We planned for her murder. If you excuse me, I now need to get onto the next portion of the plan. I will address you when I have enough information for a substantial briefing."

*"We need to get on this. You know who her parents were."*

"I do. I called them aunt and uncle, and I was next to Susa at their funeral. Now I have to plan a third."

*"I am sorry, Zera."*

"I will speak to you when I have information, Hron." She cut the call.

It was another ten minutes before she arrived at her house. She left the car and walked toward the home that was writhing with high-security personnel. She stopped in the yard and said, "I must retrieve personal and locked documents for examination by the project and teams. I require an observer to make sure that I do not remove unrecorded documentation from the house."

She heard the landing before the hand was on her shoulder.

"I will accompany her inside."

"Thank you, Astel." She headed toward the house, put the covers on her shoes, and walked into her home.

One of the investigators whispered, "Should she be in here?"

Zera kept walking.

They started in Susara's bedroom, where Zera downloaded her message centre and diary. Astel put his hand on her shoulder again. "You don't have to do this. We can go through it for you."

"You don't know what to look for."

She headed to her bedroom, where the techs were turning over her personal belongings. She ignored them and opened her tracking software. She downloaded it with Astel watching. "What is that?"

"We knew that she was in a dangerous situation, and we decided to take action. This is the action. She was tracked, her clothing was tracked, and her com was tracked. It also had an isotope bleed. I should still be able to find where they took her."

"Wait. How do you have access to all this stuff? Why is Hron so friendly with you? Is that a box of sex toys?"

Astel was easy to distract. The tech had brought the box up and opened it, staring for a moment.

Zera got up, walked around, and closed the box. "Yes. That is what they are. They were a gift from a friend who thought that since I don't get out, something should get in."

The tech snorted. "The box is still sealed."

"Nothing needed to get in." She turned her back and took her tablet.

"Astel, can you bring me to the project facilities?"

He grimaced. "Are you going to ditch me again?"

"I did not ditch you at the hospital. We were not on a date. My friend is dying, and I was trying to get her to the proper care." She sighed. "You can remain with me until your clearance runs out."

He looked abashed. "Right. Sorry."

She grabbed a bag, had him inspect it, and then, she went to her closet and took a change of clothing and got some underwear. "Do you have to inspect this as well?"

He looked at the undergarments and turned them over in his hands before returning them to her. "They are clear. Thank you for your cooperation."

"I bet that you say that every time you are in a bedroom with a lady's underthings in your hands." She smiled as she left the room. "Your mother should be proud."

"Researcher, you have a way of shoving me off balance."

She chuckled. "That is what I do. It is why I am good at my job."

She handed her bag and tablet over to the peacekeeper waiting on the outside of her house.

"Were you monitored the entire time?"

Astel nodded. "I kept Researcher Zera in my sight at all times. All downloads are what she said they are. The clothing is just a change of clothes while the investigation is ongoing."

Zera sighed but kept her mouth shut. The clothing was just so that she could appear on the newsvids and other interview events, as well as give a briefing to the teams about who they were looking for.

Her bag was handed back, and she put it across her body. Astel extended his arm, and she stepped toward him. He took off gently and carried her across the city in fifteen minutes, holding her tight against him. His suit was too well insulated to give her any body heat, but she appreciated the gesture.

She was shivering when he set her down and rubbed her arms. "Why are you being so nice?"

"Your housemate and friend was attacked, possibly fatally. You need comfort."

Zera frowned. "I do?"

He leaned in. "It is standard social response."

"Oh. I guess I am still in shock. Another standard social response." She looked at him with challenge in her expression. She knew it. She had practiced the expression in the mirror for years. "I have to go inside now."

He nodded.

"You have to let me go."

He looked down, and his hands were on her waist. "Why does this feel comfortable?"

"Because you are a fan of the curve between ribs and hips." She looked at him and kept her mind and expression blank.

He jerked his hands back. "How did . . . when . . ."

She nodded. "Please, excuse me, I have to check on Susa."

She nodded again. "Thank you for the lift."

His mouth opened and closed.

She turned and headed toward the med research building. He followed her with long strides.

"You are a program researcher. What is your designation? Even the researchers have to have some activation going on." He spoke quietly as they walked.

"Designation is classified. Consider me very smart with a lot of patience." She swiped her entry code through the first security screen, and he followed.

"Why do I remember the feel of your body?"

She felt heat in her cheeks and shrugged. "Perverse fantasy life? I am not your type, as I have heard you mention several times. You don't speak as quietly as you think you do."

He blinked. "I don't mean . . . when did I say . . . how did you hear . . ."

She snorted. "Let's just say that my activation involves enhanced senses."

"Does it?"

"No, but it is a fun thing to say." She walked through the next bio screen, and he followed.

"Why did you have Susara brought here? Why did you have her brought to the hospital first?"

"So that whoever did this to her would have the

7

satisfaction of watching her brought to the hospital and declared dead." She continued to watch and nodded to the security guards at the next gateway.

It was a little frustrating when Astel was able to stalk in after her.

"Why do you want that?"

Zera stopped and faced him in the hall. "So that the villain who did this will freak out and doubt the man who assured him her soul was gone. It will stir confusion through the ranks and drive him mad with rage."

"You have planned this." He scowled.

"We planned it. We have known it was coming for years. This is where it was always headed. This was always what would happen next."

She looked him in the eye and said, "The important thing is what happens now. So, either wait for the briefing or go elsewhere. I have to check her vitals, and then, I need to grieve the loss of my best friend."

She turned and walked through to the black sector, where Astel was not allowed to go. Sixteen people were allowed into this sector, and he wasn't one of them. There was only one team member who was allowed in, but he was across the world, dealing with the aftermath of a seismic event. That was fine. He couldn't do anything to help. No one could.

The evil bastard had set things in motion when he killed Susara's parents and then attached himself to her at the funeral. This had been his long game all along, but if everything went according to plan, they would fuck his little game six ways from sideways, and Zera would scoop out his skull and use it as a footstool.

A girl could dream.

Susa was lying in a medical gown with IVs running into her to hydrate her. The medics gave Zera the reports, and her heart sank. She walked to Susa's side, pressed Susa's hand to her forehead, and bawled like a child. There was nothing left, and the body was dying in increments.

Dr. Miliken spoke. "I know you are grieving, but we have to move. Are you ready?"

"I am. Are the backups in place?"

"They are. They are safe."

Zera gasped and wiped her tears. "Right. Can you help me get her into a chair?"

"Can't you do it like this?"

"I don't like to. Face to face is too much like sex. Are we ready?"

"Wait. We can just sit her up, and you can scoot into her that way, right?"

The bed rose, and Zera put her leg on the bed, looking at the doctor, and then, she did what she did best. She slid inside another living being.

Zera looked at her hands and flexed her fingers. "I always forget how tiny she is."

The doctor covered his mouth. "That is so disturbing."

"I know. It feels the same from this side. Send in the drone cam."

The doctor nodded and sighed. When he returned, he had a drone with him, and she smiled as the indicator went red. "Thanks to the fast work of the local team and emergency services, I am on my way to a full recovery. I hope that the people who did this to me are swiftly brought to justice." She kneaded at the blankets and smiled. "I hope I can get back to the program and up to the final assessments next week. Thanks to everyone who wished me well."

She nodded, and the bed lay back. The drone left, and she sat up. Zera got out of her best friend's body, and the tears were on her cheeks again. They left her in repose with robotic guards at the door.

It was time to do the second-best thing that she did, edit

data that should be impenetrable. It was time to set the scene and sprinkle enough truth in that people did not look too deep.

# Chapter Two

After an hour of data manipulation and compression, she was ready to explain what had happened to her friend and how long the plan had been going on.

She got up and straightened her blouse and trousers, flared her lab coat out, and headed for the briefing room on the exterior of the black zone.

The peacekeeper representatives and the team members looked at her, and she turned to the display to activate an image of Susara.

"Program elite candidate Susara, born Susara Kino and handed over to the program when she was eight. She had the tentative designation of Dainty, and her skill was best described as *Suit Bait*. She was smart, seductive, and the most amazing friend a woman can ask for. Her death was ordered by this man. The Mentor."

She flicked to a silhouette, and the men and women in the room snorted.

Hron asked, "Where would she have gotten into contact with him in the first place?"

Zera clicked the image of the funeral. "Here. She was fourteen. He came up to her and touched her cheek and shoulder. I saw him. This is my best depiction of his face."

She forwarded the image, and the group gasped.

Hron asked, "How did you see him? Why didn't you tell anyone?"

"I wasn't sure until he crossed her path again. He wanted her, wanted all her firsts. Well, the ones that were still available. He started sending her messages. She was scared, so she came to me, and we formulated a plan and a business model."

She took in a deep breath and clicked. The room dissolved in murmurs. "Since he was going to come for her anyway, she decided to draw him out. She put herself up on Blind Date and waited for him to request her. She didn't have to wait long."

Zera played the conversation.

*"Ah, little one, I want to see you in that gown with nothing under it. I am sending you the coordinates. Do you travel with a chaperone?"*

Susa's voice was soft and sexy, *"I do. One human and one mech, just in case. They are circumspect and will remain within five hundred metres of me during the entire encounter. After the designated hour, they will come in and look for me if I am not outside. They will find me."*

*"A charming threat. I will be on my best behaviour."*

*"I will have my mask, but what shall I call you, sir?"*

*"Consider me your mentor and address me as such."*

The call disconnected, and Susa's voice asked, *"Did you get that, Zera?"*

*"Yes, Dainty."*

*"Well, Hopper, suit up. He took the bait. You are my ride."*

They both chuckled, and the call ended.

Zera sighed. "The meetings started through the app, and I came with her to every one. The security bot came with us, and she got more and more information on the Mentor. Then, he started booking her for hours at a time. He started to involve others in their encounters, and that is how she met the man she fell in love with and he with her. Their boss was informed, and she ended up an empty shell. The man who did this was Jinthen Vel, the doll maker."

The peacekeeper captain asked, "How do you know what she did with her clients?"

"She told me, but more than that, I was along for the ride. She told me about every meeting and took me along on every trip until last night."

"What was different about last night?" Hron asked.

"Delvis was going to die. Apparently, the Mentor would bring him in for a threesome but was upset when Dainty preferred him."

One of the researchers looked at her in surprise. "What do you mean, *along for the ride*, Hopper?"

Hron frowned. "You have an activation, Hopper?"

"I can enter the mind of others, whether they want to or not. I was holding her hand—metaphorically speaking—on every date."

Hron cleared his throat. "You are bound by the blindness as well?"

"Of these little masks?" she tossed one to the boardroom table. "Of course not. I designed them; I can override them. Don't worry. My staff can't."

The team members relaxed. The peacekeepers were curious, and the captain asked, "What the hell is Blind Date?"

"Escorts for the activated. It is legal. I have all necessary permits." Zera smiled. "Women and men who disclose their vulnerabilities and are excellent lovers for those who are in stressful private positions."

The peacekeepers looked at each other in surprise. Hron filled in, "It is a lovely time but hellishly expensive."

One of the peacekeepers put the mask on. It adhered to his face, and he panicked. Zera walked up to him as the scanners rejected him, and the mask dropped back into her hands. "It isn't calibrated for you. It won't stay on."

"I just saw blurry figures."

"Yeah, that is all it allows you to see. Even I can only get thermal data."

Astel blinked. "You do this as well?"

Naima smiled, "Can I get your number?"

Zera smiled. "You have already had it. Most of the teams that come here work their way through the roster. The personnel I have will service either sex, so it works very equitably."

Naima frowned. "I don't remember you."

Zera nodded. "It is on our contract. Your short-term memory will be blurred as to specific details, but you will retain all the bulk memories of your contracted time. Shape, size, sounds, but not voices."

Astel looked at her in shock. She shrugged.

The captain asked, "Why would they pay for that?"

Hron met her gaze and answered, "Because Zera knows that we have trouble finding lovers who are activated and won't be injured and who aren't seeking us out for fame or popularity. It is once and done." He chuckled. "Until we realize how freeing it is, and then, we do it again."

Naima sighed, "And again and again."

Zera gripped her mask. "I would like the record to show that the team members stated that they were clients and not me."

Hron chuckled, "So noted."

Astel smiled slightly, and Naima blew her a kiss.

Zera looked to the peacekeepers. "As you are suddenly aware, the activation also works on the hormones, pheromones, and sex drive. You can't have enjoyable sex if you would tear through your partner like gauze. The teams have to either look for other activated folks or remain celibate." She sighed. "The activated crime bosses have the same issue."

The peacekeepers' eyes widened. "You service *them*?"

Zera shrugged. "Sure. It would look weird if we only serviced team members and would not be much of a business. As it is, we are very successful."

She turned back to the briefing and explained, "Right, if that little verbal voyeurism is over, there is a vid going out this evening that is a thank you from Susa. I need to make

14

sure that you all act as if it is a truth."

Dr. Miliken stood up. "The file is queued up."

Zera caught the video and saw her sliding into the sitting body of Susa. She grimaced. "I told you not to use internal cameras for this."

Dr. Miliken blushed. "I will have them disabled."

Zera gritted her teeth as she puppeted Susa to say what she needed to. The drone footage was next up. It was a repeat with a better angle.

She slowly turned back to the people gathered. She sighed. "So, *that* is my activation, and now, you know that the name Hopper does not involve me skipping in and out of beds."

The team members were standing and staring at her. Naima whispered, "You made her talk."

"No, I was talking. My cells were mingled with her cells. When she sat up, that was me sitting up. I phase in and then can either ride along or take over. Then I hop out." She sighed. "At the point she recorded that message, she weighed nearly one hundred and twenty-five kilos."

The team was staring at her. Hron looked at her, down to his com, and then up again with a slight smile.

She felt the haptic pulse through her com and glanced down. If she was amenable, she had a three-hour date for that evening. She scowled and pressed *accept*. Details of what she should wear would be forwarded to her. There was an online collection to choose from.

She sighed and turned. "So, this is the security camera footage from the surrounding area." She watched the man blur into the screen, set her down, and kiss her temple with tears tracking down his cheek. "And that is Delvis. He isn't going to be my way in, but he is an ally once I get there."

He arranged her carefully into the seated position and disappeared. The next image was Zera rolling up and taking her into her arms, wailing. To Zera's surprise, the ground shook around her and Susa while she rocked and waited for the peacekeepers.

Astel leaned forward. "You called everyone before you arrived?"

"Before I left the house. When I got up, instead of being ready for a run, I found this in her room."

Susara's voice rang out, slurring and giggling. *"Zera, today's the day. Delvis said he was going to tell the boss that we are in love. It has been so long, and I am so tired, but I am sure about Delvis. I know that he wants to take care of me and doesn't have loyalty to the boss. When he touches me . . . Hopper, it isn't like anyone else I have ever touched."* There was another drunken giggle. *"So, I know this is going to freak you out, but I will be home soon, and then, you can yell at me for going out without an escort. Love you, Zera."*

Zera inhaled and exhaled slowly. "So, that was the last thing Dainty sent me. I activated all trackers and the isotope reader and sent emergency services. I honestly hoped that she was beaten nearly to death, but that wasn't the case."

That shocked the law enforcement in the room, but the researchers nodded. Dr. Miliken sighed. "We can heal physical damage."

Understanding dawned.

"So, I propose that we find the doll maker, find Mentor, and remove both of their heads for research purposes." She smiled brightly. "Any questions?"

The men and women looked at each other uneasily. One of the peacekeepers asked, "How can you say that so cheerfully?"

Hron smiled, his eyes glowing icy blue. "Because she is Researcher Zera. She tackles one problem at a time, and now, these men have become a problem, so she is going to solve it."

Her cheeks got a little pink when she saw Torun's gaze looking at her through Hron's eyes. She checked her com when it pulsed and saw that the empress outfit had been requested. Torun was on his way to town.

She looked at Hron and asked, "How long have you been in there, Torun?"

Her friend's slow smile was wicked. "Long enough."

The room turned to stare at Hron and the star-bright eyes.

The captain asked, "Torun, what do you think of her plan?"

He smiled. "I think she is going to do it regardless of what we say or do. So, if we want her to come out of this alive—and we do—it is up to us to simply ask the question." He leaned forward on his elbows. "Zera, what do you need from us?"

Part of her soul melted. He always knew just what to say. "I will need the researchers to continue on their end of the project."

They nodded.

"I will need the peacekeepers to be willing to work with me for the final investigation, and if I call the team, I would like them to arrive without a barrage of questions." She straightened. "I will be appearing primarily as Susa over the next week. Mentor always watches the challenges and testing. He considers it recruitment advertising."

Astel frowned. "You are going to wear her body for the testing?"

"I am. I will request confidential testing, which will also give us a trail when Mentor tries to break into Susa's file."

Torun laughed. "You are leading him along."

"His need to solve puzzles is incredible. He has to be smarter than anyone else in the room, or he has them killed, and he is going to be hunting doll maker the moment that I am seen at the testing grounds. Since Susa will obviously be alive and pass the challenges, everyone will be watching her. I will need the research team to be there on testing day. I am only two candidates behind her, so I will need someone to take her somewhere safe after I step out."

The research team nodded. "We will be there doing checks on the students. We can simply divert her after the exam."

"I will retrieve her and walk her out after I am done with my own testing."

Torun smiled. "You are joining a team?"

"Oh, god, no. I don't have a socially serving bone in my body. I am trained for research, but I have to maintain my credentials to continue working on team accessories. I need to keep my rating up so that I can experiment with the weapons on myself."

He blinked, the bright glow of his eyes getting stronger. "You can withstand our weaponry?"

One of the researchers snorted. "Of course, she can take them point-blank. She designed them all."

Zera looked at him. "Torun, how close are you?"

There was a slight scuff of his boots, and she turned around slowly. He let Hron loose and inclined his head. His purple skin with jagged lightning marks was her favourite colour. The suit that he was wearing was a deep blue that was nearly black. His hair was held off his face with a thick clasp at the base of his neck so that the rest of his locks hung down to mid-back.

He stepped toward her. "I am pretty close."

She looked up and up again. His eyes held her hypnotized, and it took an effort to look away.

Hron unintentionally came to her rescue. "Torun, how long are you in the city?"

She was easing away and froze when he said, "Overnight. I will be taking meetings in the morning before rejoining my team."

She took a step away from him. "Right. So, that's it. I am going to lure some evil people out into the open and then kill them. I just wanted you all to know because I will need witnesses regarding my unhinged state of mind at this particular stage."

One of the peacekeepers frowned. "Unhinged?"

It appeared that they needed a demonstration. She picked up the boardroom table, scattering the group, and she smashed it down with a scream before going and punching the smart glass.

Torun grabbed her from behind and lifted her off her feet. He murmured softly, "They get the point."

He carried her into one of the nearby offices, and when the door was locked, he whispered, "I am so sorry about Susara."

She exhaled, inhaled, and started sobbing, his arms holding her arms down and supporting her around her ribs. This wasn't the crying of shock, the weeping of grief; this was the acknowledgement that half her soul was gone.

Torun held her while she wailed and didn't mention that she was shaking the walls.

When she quieted, he set her down in a chair and then left. He returned a moment later with a cold cloth for her eyes. "Easy, Zera. That was a lot to get out."

She mumbled her thanks and spent the next few minutes cooling her eyes until she could see out of them again. Crying blood when truly upset had only happened once before, when Susa's parents were murdered.

Torun was crouching in front of her, and when she looked at him, he smiled sadly. "You should have called me."

"You were busy with work. I told you back then that I would never step between you and duty."

"You did, but I also told you that I would come when you call."

She smiled slightly.

"Dirty girl. That too, but you have the right to make demands on me."

"Um, no, I don't. We are not exclusive." She used his phrasing.

"This business of yours was my suggestion. I know that you need more, but I can't always provide it. The few times that we have gotten together with my team have been . . . memorable." His eyes went hot. "However, you and I alone have been the moments I look forward to. I come back here far more than I should, and I don't regret anything."

He stroked her cheek, and she leaned her head into the touch. "You are an expensive habit, Zera."

She swallowed. "That was never my intention."

"No, but it has highlighted a need to the project. The Blind Dates are actually a budget point for the teams. We are more effective as a team if we can get what we need from a scheduled servicing." He smiled. "Also, we are far more friendly to those we are assisting."

Zera looked at him with narrowed eyes. "How friendly?"

"Jealous?"

"Yes. Being greedy is one of my characteristics. You know that."

He chuckled and exhaled slowly, his eyes warming again. "Yes, I definitely do. It is one of your more endearing characteristics."

She asked him. "How secure is that lock?"

He smiled. "Pretty secure. Why?"

"I need a little more comforting that won't get you out of your suit."

"Pity." He caught her and got to his feet as she held his face and kissed him as if he was the last man in the world.

She pressed the cold cloth to her lips and sighed. "Sorry for mauling you."

He was leaning against the desk with her cuddled against him, his hand smoothing over her back.

His eyes crackled with power. "I will pay you back this evening."

She blushed and checked her com. "Eleven hours?" She blinked. The money was astronomical. "Is the rest of the team coming or something?"

He chuckled. "They wanted to come, but we voted that I would be the one to represent us. If things work out tonight, I will be able to invite them along for their favourite parts."

She shivered at the thought, and he stroked her cheek. "I think that you are ready to return to the meeting now. For what it's worth, you have thought it out to a frightening degree. How long will Susa's body hold up?"

She sighed and ran a hand through her hair. "Two weeks at the outside. I can supplement her when I am inside her."

"Now, serious question. Did you ever go with her to Mentor as a date?"

She nodded. "Twice. It was a party for a new associate and some kind of an anniversary."

"Did you do any hopping?"

She chuckled. "A little. That is how I knew the doll maker's work when I saw it. I know that he *can* hold onto the soul, but if he wants to, it is something completely different."

He hugged her. "Did any of them hurt you?"

She wrinkled her nose. "There were no permanent injuries. Soft tissue heals quickly. For me, more so than others. You also know that hurting me does not mean that I didn't have a good time."

"It is one of your more worrying and endearing qualities." He chuckled and stroked her hair. "You look good dressed for work. If you add a baton to the ensemble, I will request it for the next time."

She swallowed. "You can still change it."

"No, I want to see you in all your glory, my empress."

"But, eleven hours?"

"You need contact, and I want contact, and I want to hold you when you wake."

She exhaled slowly. "Fine. Have you chosen your hotel?"

"The Zephr. I will send you the room number when I

have checked in. I will expect you at seven."

He set her on her feet, stroked her back, and walked into the boardroom without her. She checked the time and groaned. It wasn't even noon yet.

# Chapter Three

Dr. Miliken looked at her as she ran her numbers. "So, you and Torun . . ."

"He's a client. The service was his idea when he and I first got together. There hadn't been any specifically scheduled relief for quite some time, and no one was recruiting for this branch of service. So, Blind Date was created, and he was the first, second, and third client before the others started asking him about why he was relaxed and more even-tempered and more powerful. From there, it expanded, and I ended up with my little roster of program students and one professor."

The doctor asked, "Really?"

"Two of the team members have maturity interests, so I had to go recruiting." She chuckled. "And that is the last of the gossip regarding the Blind Date Corporation."

"But, you know all this stuff."

"I do."

"And you and your escorts are not considered a threat?"

"The folk who work for me have the same vague memories as their clients. The masks interfere with the electronics around them. It is a frequency of my own discovery." She smiled. "I own the patent on the projector."

"The program doesn't own it?"

"No. I created it when I was sixteen. Dr. Yamel helped me file the patent." She continued to check the data with the location triangulation. She compared all of the date data and came up with one annoying conclusion. Mentor was using a portal, and she hadn't even noticed. "Well, fuck."

She had been so fixated on keeping an eye on Susa that she hadn't bothered to check if Mentor was using volatile technology that could have ripped them apart. She frowned. It wasn't like her to miss that.

Zera was frowning over the data when her com chimed an alarm. "Aw, hell. Right. I am going for the day. Notify me if anything changes in Susa's condition. I might not answer immediately, but I will be checking in every few hours."

"Where are you going?"

"First, I am kissing Susa goodnight, and then, I am going home." She locked down her terminal and got up.

"I thought you had more research to do."

"There is always more research to do. Now, I have to uphold my obligations."

"You don't mean . . ."

"Don't wait up."

She headed to Susara's room, checked her monitors, her vitals, and then pressed a soft kiss to her forehead. "Behave. I will be back in the morning with stories to tell if you want to listen, just like old times. Tonight's client asked for the full empress, so you know how much work that is going to be. You always hated doing that one."

She smoothed the pale hair back and got up. She said she was heading home, but in reality, she was going to the offices of Blind Date Corporation. That is where all of the equipment was to fulfill the requests of the clients and where all dates began and ended.

The empress was an intricate costume born of the history of Torun's people. There was apparently an empress who would get ready for her lovers and challenge them to please her or die. The costume was tricky and meant she would have to remove all hair from the chin down and do some serious grooming to her eyebrows. The enema was pretty standard by this point.

The stand-up hair remover did the entire job in under five minutes.

It was time to get pretty.

After the layers of scraped skin, makeup, and intricate designs, she had a quick snack before putting on the gauzy silk layers that only concealed in the same way cobwebs were concealing. There were two other escorts getting ready, and when they heard what she was gearing up for, they expressed their sympathies at her prep routine.

Twelve was going to visit a businessman for a scenario that involved a little hunting and chasing. Three was off for an evening of a private concert and some straightforward sex with another non-team client.

One had to go and put on ten pounds of jewels, her customized mask for this costume, and a headdress that fit over the mask. When she was done, the bots wrapped her in the cloak and she stepped onto the footpads that would ease her walk. She had listened to the news while she got ready, and Torun's team had been seen landing at a nearby base.

Her maintenance bot and guard bot accompanied her to the transport. Through the mask, she looked out at the people on the street going on dates, dances, and heading out for dinner. She was doing one of those things, but the difference in her night was that it was guaranteed to end in sex unless the client changed their minds. In the six years of the company, only one client had changed their mind, and it was because they were summoned to attend an emergency. They rescheduled as soon as they were able, and Susa had had a very nice time.

The transport glided to a halt, and her bots preceded her. She did not let the doorman take her hand. She had the code for clearance past the guard and for the private elevator.

The guard muttered as her bots rolled into the lift with

her, "What kind of a whore are you?"

She smiled slightly. "I work with a niche clientele. Good evening."

The lift took her upward, and her guardian bot remained outside the doors, making sure that anyone who arrived was allowed to be there. On this floor level, there were only four doors. The odds were slim that anyone would sneak in.

Her maintenance bot came with her, ready to repair her makeup over the course of the evening. They would take breaks, and the makeup would be repaired and replaced as often as needed.

Zera tried to ignore the flutter in her belly as she held the icon programmed with the location, and the third door lit up. She walked to the door, and it opened at her approach. The maintenance bot proceeded her and took up a station near the door.

She walked in precisely on time to see Torun lounging on a couch in his casual gear. A wrap made of black silk covered his hips, and nothing else covered the purple expanse of his body. She could not see it in colour, but she could imagine it. She unlaced her cloak and pushed the hood back carefully. She went into a deep curtsy and asked, "Is everything as my patron wishes?"

He slowly got up and slid the cloak away from her, tossing it to one side. "Oh. Yes. This is perfect. You have outdone yourself, One. Are you okay with this?"

She nodded. "I need the distraction, and you are definitely distracting, Patron."

She went back into character. "Are you willing to please your empress?"

Zera saw the curve of his lips a moment before he traced the first design around her lips with his tongue. She had three hundred patterns on her, and they would only dissolve with saliva.

He went after each pattern with intensity, and as he knelt to lave his tongue over her collarbone and breasts, she felt the slight trickle of honey on her inner thighs. He paused in his quest and leaned toward her waist. "My empress, it seems that you have an urgent need."

He idly trailed his fingers up her inner thigh.

She swallowed. "I would not call it urgent."

He slid two fingers into her and tasted them. "Your heat is surprising in one of your status."

"Alleviate it then, and I shall begin again."

He laughed and got to his feet, lifting her high in the air before bringing her down his body. He reached between them, and his erection fit against her until he pulled her onto him in a brutal shove that would have torn anyone who wasn't activated with a physical adaptation. She wrapped her legs around him as he withdrew and thrust hard; their bodies bucked and twisted, and she let her upper body fall back until he caught her with both hands and thrust while his mouth sucked and nipped at her breasts. She was his, totally and without reservation, and as his cock thrust inside her, she bucked and groaned, clawing at his arms as her first climax hit hard. He held himself inside her and grunted as he jetted inside her for his first time that evening: ten hours and forty minutes to go.

He pulled her up face to face, and his kiss scorched her soul. The gems clashed as theirs was less of a kiss and more of a consumption. She held his head and kissed him and felt the tears seeping through her mask.

"Aw, baby. Don't cry. I am not that pretty."

She chuckled and nipped at his lip. "I wish that I could see you, but that isn't in the contract."

"We know who you are, Zera, and you know who we are. You can forego the mask with us."

"We are the only ones in here." She checked to make sure she was correct."

"The others are waiting in the next room. I just have to give them the word. We were going to do this by transfer, but we all want to feel you at once."

She shuddered. "How many are we talking about?"

He traced her lower lip with his tongue. "Just the four of us. Me, you, Ryma, Tycho."

She shuddered again. "They can come in. Should I reset?"

"Please. It is more fun if we can all start at the same time."

Zera swallowed and removed her mask. "Then, I had better get off your cock and get started. Please, warn them that sex without the mask is a lot more sarcastic."

He nuzzled her cheek. "Just like old times."

She laughed and pressed her hands to his shoulders, moving off him with some difficulty. He wasn't helping at all. She dropped to the ground and looked at his erection. "That was quick."

"Around you, my empress, it is a continual state."

She blushed and went to the maintenance bot. It expanded into a shower-style cubicle, and she was cleaned of cum, and her designs were repainted. Everything was on a base layer of gold, and the base layer only came off with a specific solvent. She was going to be getting gold off her vulva for days.

It took her five minutes to reset. When she stepped out, Torun drew her to his side as the door opened and Ryma and Tycho came in.

They stopped when they were inside and wearing what Zera considered to be orgy clothing. A scrap of wrap on Tycho and a chiffon tunic on Ryma. They both looked wonderful, but then, the teams always did.

"I am terribly overdressed." Zera smiled.

Ryma walked up to her and kissed her. "You look wonderful."

Tycho kissed her when Ryma moved aside. "Torun said he took the edge off, so we can play."

Zera looked at him. "Is that what that was? The edge? I thought I got the whole thing."

He swatted her backside, the other two laughed, and there was just one thing she had to ask, "You are alright with me going without the mask?"

Tycho smiled. "I have wanted to see your eyes for years, Zera."

"I had no idea that they were hazel." Ryma smiled. "I always thought they would be brown."

"Most folks can't tell the difference."

Torun smiled. "The green and purple in the jewellery make the colours more distinct."

Zera quirked her lips. "Now, do I have to play damsel in distress, or can I just turn myself over to your hands and bodies?"

Torun chuckled. "I don't think we have ever had you play a person in distress. We get enough of that with the day job."

She looked to Ryma and smiled. "What about a game of tag one day? If you are interested, I run, and you hunt."

Ryma made a fist in Zera's hair, pulling her head back. Her eyes were shining, and there was excitement in them. "That sounds like fun. But, would you enjoy it, little rabbit? I know that I am not your preferred prey."

"Ah, making you happy is its own type of enjoyment. Name the date; I'll bring the toybox." Making casual conversation while having your neck exposed to a fanged predator had taken some getting used to.

Ryma kissed her savagely. "I look forward to it."

She returned the kiss. Females were not her preference, but her preference didn't matter. Pleasure mattered. Giving and receiving were high on her list. The teams were monsters; the criminals were monsters. Her entire world was full of scary monsters. She should know. She was one of them.

She heard a groan, and Tycho knelt next to her hip, his tongue tracing a design that arrowed directly toward her groin. His fingers crept up her inner thigh, and she gasped.

29

Torun cupped her breasts and traced his tongue over a design on her neck and shoulder. When Tycho's tongue entered her, her legs buckled. This was his favourite thing to do, and Torun supported her while massaging and pinching her breasts to stiff peaks.

Ryma straddled one of her thighs and sucked at one nipple while grinding against her. Zera caught her hand and sucked her fingers. Ryma shuddered and groaned as Zera swirled her tongue around and around. The feral team member grunted and whimpered as Zera's thigh was slick.

Tycho was persistent in his activities, and when he slid his third finger in and rapidly flicked her clit with his tongue, she twisted in Torun's grip and arched hard against the invasion and the fluttering tongue. The sound she made was harsh and raw, causing the team around her to chuckle softly as they returned to work on the designs and patterns.

She yowled and sobbed in frustration as they made a game out of how many designs they could eradicate with their tongues. Tycho provided the manacles that they used to hang her from a hook in the ceiling while they worked. She was up on her toes as they turned her from left to right and back again.

Only nine hours and twenty minutes to go.

# Chapter Four

Zera groaned, and a hand stroked her hair; someone kissed her temple. She was at the bottom of a very tangled pile of limbs of mixed colourations. Her body was telling her it was time to get up for her run, but her contract was going to keep her pinned for the next hour.

Torun moved his teammates off her and eased her under him. She thought he was going to speak, but he kissed her, and his thigh parted hers. Zera shuddered and opened her legs for him so that he could just slide in. He stretched her to aching as he moved inside her. His slow undulations into her touched every nerve.

He kissed her tenderly, moving inside her with little of the frenzy from the previous night. The bite marks on her breasts, belly, and shoulders were already healing. The marks on her inner thighs where Tycho had drunk her blood stung, but it made the slow thrusts that Torun was treating her to all the sweeter. He took every gasp, every moan, and gave her soft sighs and low growls.

She stroked her arms up his sides and held him tight as he pushed into her and retreated. He murmured against her mouth, "You are still so fucking tight."

She blushed and muttered, "And you are still too fucking big."

He grinned and increased the speed and depth of his thrusts. She planted her feet flat on the bed, and the tension in her muscles made it tighter, harder for him to move.

"You play dirty, Zera."

"I play dirty? I am not the one who spent two hours last night shoving himself into my ass." She muttered it, and it

31

ended on a gasp as her body convulsed under his. Her body felt like liquid gold as he continued to rock into it.

He laughed. "Every part of you is mine, and it is my generosity that shares you with the other teams."

"Big words when you have me pinned."

"Ah, but I have you right where I want you." He dragged his tongue up her neck. "And I want all of you that I can get. It might be a while before I am back in town."

She kissed him again, holding his head. "I had forgotten how pretty your eyes were when you cum."

He growled, and his blue-white eyes glowed as he pounded into her, the power radiating from them as he focused on her features. He shoved deep, and his neck corded with effort as he jerked into her. His cock flexed and pulsed before he let out a groan and slowly collapsed on her. She wrapped her arms and legs around him and held him tight until the shuddering and twitching stopped. She sighed and licked his ear. She ran her nails up his spine, and he shuddered and plunged into her again.

Tycho was on his elbow, watching with a fascinated expression. "How do you know how to do that?"

Torun chuckled, his voice husky. "Yeah, Zera, how do you know how to do that?"

"Um. Trial and error. Torun and I have danced before."

Ryma leaned up behind Tycho. "You call that dancing?"

She smiled. "It is as close as I have come to it."

Tycho's face was shocked. "What?"

She chuckled. "I am a busy woman. I don't have time for dancing."

Torun laughed. "Busy indeed. Here I am still balls deep in you, and you are talking about dancing."

Zera slowly undulated her hips. "Isn't this dancing? I have a partner, we are close, and there is a rhythm."

He smiled slowly. "You aren't going to be able to walk today."

"Oh, baby, that ship has sailed."

He rolled, and she rode him slowly; a flicker in his eyes told her what was coming next or, rather, who. Tycho and his ridiculous amounts of precum slid into her ass as Torun pulled her toward him.

She felt her eyes widen as she whined softly as Tycho forged forward. Torun smiled. "That is what I have been missing. Seeing the enjoyment, confusion, and lack of control is intoxicating."

Zera tried to shift her hips between them, and she was pinned. She sighed. "One of you is going to have to move. I am pinned."

Tycho cupped her breasts and shifted. "I think that is my cue."

She groaned and panted as he moved inside her, and Torun watched with his eyes glowing hot. He was getting secondary effect, but the effect was that she was rhythmically contracting and releasing him as Tycho's cock rubbed his through her.

She shivered, Tycho shouted, and Torun arched back. They withdrew to clean up, and Ryma took over. She held Zera and used warm water and a soft cloth to take care of her. This was the part that Ryma didn't get in her daily life. She wanted to care for helpless things, but she was relegated to the part of the beast. Zera let a few tears fall as Ryma cleaned her with detailed care. Susa used to help with aftercare on nights like this, but now, Zera would be left to the bots. This was the only care she would get.

Zera would have normally protested the help with the solvent to remove the gold, but Ryma was careful, and she worked with the prep bot to get it all off. When she was clean, rubbed down with lotion, and the worst aches had been massaged, Zera hugged the team member in thanks.

"You are off the clock, Zera."

Zera nodded against her shoulder. "I know." She straightened her shoulders and put her cloak and the mask back on.

Torun was putting on his team uniform. "Why are you bothering with that?"

"Because I know you have doxed me with the teams, but I want to avoid it getting out any further than necessary, or you guys won't get any more energy weapons." She smiled. "I am heading into commuter traffic. My transport is pulling up." She bowed. "Thank you, Patrons, for selecting me."

They each gave her a whisper of a kiss. Ryma smiled. "Thank you for taking care of us."

Tycho smiled. "Thank you for taking care of us." He pressed another kiss to her lips.

Torun pulled her close and growled. "Thank you for taking care of us."

His kiss was not quick, was not delicate, and left her knees shaking and her monitor chiming that her transport was waiting.

Her lips were swollen, and he stroked her cheek. "See you soon, Zera."

She blinked, and then, his words sank in. "Wait. How soon?"

A laughing Tycho steered her toward the lift, pulled her cloak up, and kissed her cheek. "Goodbye, Zera. Have a nice day at work. We will."

That was all the warning she got as the doors closed and she was transported to the lobby. She walked out with her bots and headed to her transport. It opened for her when she was four feet away, much to the irritation of a businessman who was trying to pry it open. He hurled epithets at her while her guard bot kept him at bay and the maintenance bot came inside with her. When her guard joined her, she settled back into an exhausted doze until she was at home base. Now, she had to get dressed for work. She was *not* wearing pants today. The pressure would drive her crazy.

She took a final shower to get rid of the last residual

DNA and got two protein bars and some hot tea while she flicked through the wardrobe that was available. She opted for a long navy-blue wrap dress with short sleeves. The low-heeled shoes that matched had straps that walked them up the calves, which meant no need for stockings. She had to use a breast band, but that was her only concession to undergarments.

It was as loose as she could go without going naked. She shivered at that thought and checked her schedule. She summoned her transport and grabbed her tablet. It was time to leave the safety of the base and head to work. Susa would love to hear about what had gone on the previous night. She had rarely taken on a team, and it seemed to be Zera's niche market.

She checked to make sure that her appearance was unremarkable and headed out to the program compound with her multi-com on her wrist. She looked just like every other woman walking to catch her ride. When her transport showed up, she was a little worried. She was attracting a bit more attention on the street than she normally did. The wind blew, and her skirt ruffled. The breeze cooled her hot thighs, and she had the odd thought that she should have worn a slip.

Zera walked into the program building, where her friend Alya smiled. "You are looking rather pretty today. Not wearing your hair up?"

"Oh, shit. That's it. Thanks, Alya."

"That is what?"

"Why I have been feeling off today." She sighed. "I was getting a lot of looks on the street."

"Are you going to be in the briefing in ten?"

"Yup. I just have to say hello to Susa, and then, I will be right up. Main boardroom?"

"Amphitheatre."

"Shit. I will be there in thirteen minutes. Save me a seat?"

"Will you leave your hair down?"

She snorted. "Yes."

"Then, yes. But I am sitting up at the front."

"Shit. Well, I hope that others are late."

"That is doubtful."

"Why?"

"Check your itinerary. See you in thirteen minutes."

Zera looked at the itinerary and bolted down to Susa, kissed her forehead, and said, "Love you; yesterday was fun and weird. I think I am heading toward another shift, and I don't have you to talk me through it. This one is strange, though; there seems to be an attraction component like the one you used but different. Okay, I am late for a meeting, but I want to discuss this with you later."

She kissed Susa's forehead again and headed up into the lift with a few other researchers heading toward the briefing. When she arrived, Alya was standing in the front row, waving frantically.

Zera walked down to the front of the amphitheatre, where it seemed every professor and student who was involved in a research team was present.

Dr. Miliken started the briefing on time.

"Despite the events of yesterday, the program goes on, and our testing and recruitment phase is beginning. Some of you have already declared your specialities, and some of you have been in your chosen occupation for decades. Today, you are going to be briefed on what your options are regarding your future."

Zera blinked as the team research group came forward. She sat up and listened to their pitch on research to work with and benefit the teams specifically. There were speeches given by folk in the economics industry, think tanks, public service, private sector applications, and then the teams arrived. The first team was familiar. Hron, Naima, and Astel talked about local service and the benefits of working with your own people; while Torun, Ryma, and

Tycho spoke about natural disasters, stellar events, and the occasional dip into their world's history.

As the other speakers had before, they threw the room open to questions. Zera crossed her legs, and Tycho's gaze focused on her limbs. He had been in the middle of a sentence and had paused. She blushed and quickly uncrossed her legs, tucking them together, but that caused her wrap dress to slide open, and she grabbed the drape that was trying to get away while she kept her hand on her knee and her expression bland.

Torun was grinning, and Ryma was covering her smile with her hand while Tycho got himself back under control and answered the question about duty shifts and time for personal activities.

Someone raised their hand, and when Tycho nodded, they said, "I have been hearing rumours about the teams using an escort agency for sex partners, and do you have any information on how someone can apply?"

Zera's eyes went wide, and she pressed her lips together.

Tycho coughed and said, "Yes, we do use an agency. Tech is involved so that we don't see them and they don't see us. That way, our preferences are kept discreet. Of course, all of the escorts are under non-disclosure agreements, but they can't remember who they were with either."

One of the men raised their hand and said, "What is the fun in that? If you can't remember them, how do you know if you enjoyed yourself or not?"

Ryma put her hand on Tycho's shoulder and spoke. "What if you had a physical activation and you could not find a sexual partner once your training completed? You try things but are worried about injury or worse for your lover. When the corporation started up, Torun was the first client, and when his escort didn't bend or break, he recommended it to others. His testing process was thorough, I am sure. I have never had a bad date since, and my emotional outlook has dramatically improved." She smiled. "When your activation takes over, you are afraid of your own body. When you first try to reach out for contact, you seek friendship, but then, you seek a lover, which is when things go wrong. Your fangs pop at the last minute; your claws are too sharp. In the case of the guys, one craves blood at the wrong moment, and the other can screw his lover through a wall if he isn't careful, which means he has to always be careful, which means sex is stressful."

"When we join the program, we give up our family names and our families to keep them safe, but we give up a lot more. You have already given it up just by being here. Now, imagine a life not knowing the touch of someone who cares, with no end in sight."

The gathered people murmured, and a coy woman asked, "Do you always use the same person?"

"The same escort? No. They each specialize, so we can choose by mood. If I wish someone to dote on, I select that person. If I need a bit more of a fight, I choose someone else."

That made them blink, but she showed her canines, and some of the super-keen women flinched. Her preference for ladies was well known, and she chuckled. "See? Not as easy as one might imagine."

Torun took the podium. "As I have been involved with the Blind Date Corporation since before its inception, I can field any additional questions. First, I believe you are curious as to how to apply, and the first step is to fill out an application on the app."

Zera looked at him, and she was scowling. *Don't do it. Don't you fucking do it.*

"As for personal experience, I believe that Zera could fill you in on the details of the service."

The room got very quiet, and then, it got very loud. Tycho extended his hand to her, and she lifted out of her chair and floated onto the stage. His telekinesis was a side effect of his activation into a blood drinker.

She stalked over to the podium and elbowed Torun out of the way. He was snorting with laughter. "Asshole."

The gathered folk were concerned and gasping.

She held up her hand. "So, before anyone gets their panties in a bunch, I am going to just say that the program and the teams' administration accept the Blind Date Corporation as a legitimate branch of activated employment. It is unorthodox and not widely accepted, but matching a team member or activated member of the public is tricky if anyone is hiding something."

She pinched the bridge of her nose. "Questions?"

A forest of hands shot up. She pointed to one of the women who had already spoken. "Yes?"

"How did you get into it?"

She shrugged. "Torun suggested it. As many of you know, my activation has come with certain emotional distancing issues, so when Torun and I became lovers, he asked me if I would consider offering myself to another team member in need of a lover." She shrugged. "I said yes and then joined Blind Date Corporation."

Another hand went up. "How many lovers have you had, and do you get tested?"

She blinked. "Ah. Well, I have lovers from both the teams and simply activated persons in a variety of occupations. Before they are allowed to access our database, they have to provide genetic fingerprinting and a blood sample analyzed at our lab, not theirs. From there, an extensive psychological profile is created, and they are monitored for no less than eight weeks, regardless of occupation."

She took a deep breath. "After they are authorized, they are given a limited selection of dates to choose from. The ones that can take the most damage. The delicates are held back until three dates have been accomplished with no physical injury or undue force. The escorts on those dates are doing the character analysis and an estimate of the propensity for violence. Some of the escorts don't mind a bit of violence now and then, but when they ask for a client to be removed from their roster, they are. Both escort and client are tested every three months if they want to remain listed with the company."

Next question. "Do the clients ask for the same escorts time after time?"

She shook her head. "No, they can select anyone available on their menu. If they want to go for a run in the moonlight, it is a different selection than when they just want a sweaty tangle of limbs. Some of the ladies or gentlemen who enjoy sex are not really that athletic."

A burst of laughter rushed through the audience.

She nodded to the next hand in the air. "Have you ever had to fire a client? If so, what were the circumstances."

Zera paused before she answered. "Yes."

"What were the circumstances?"

She took a deep breath. "He tried to kill me." She felt the tension in the men and women around her. "He lied on his application, sent someone else's DNA profile and scans. I did the initial scan of him when we met, and he punched me. I woke up with him on top of me, strangling me with enough force to break a light post, and I struck him. I called the local peacekeepers, and they had no interest in following up, so I called a team while I hid in the bathroom and typed my situation. He made it through the door a moment before help arrived, and I survived the night with my neck crushed. My voice returned three days later. New protocols were put in place immediately, involving the intensive verifying of the clients."

The room was silent. "So, it isn't just screwing your favourite teams. It is a legitimate danger to your person. This is a chance to make a lot of money, but you can also lose your life, your health, your true love. Never fall in love with a client. That is why the masks are an issue. Only management knows who your client actually is and what they want. They have to outline things with management, and you can decide if that pushes your limits. You then get a list of things to do to prep for the date, preferred hairstyle, makeup, body hair, or not. They have a catalogue of outfits to choose from."

One of the men in her department raised his hand. She knew where this was going.

"What are your limits?"

Torun laughed. "We will let you know if we find them."

The crowd was murmuring *we?* Zera winced when Torun kissed her hand, Tycho kissed her neck, and Ryma licked her other palm.

The room burst into astonished roars.

# Chapter Five

When Dr. Miliken entered the space, he gestured for everyone to quiet. "Ladies and gentlemen, please be quiet. I understand that our unscheduled speaker is fascinating, but you need to keep your self-control. If Researcher Zera is willing, I am sure that you will all get your questions answered. If you are interested in hearing more, please notify the organizers, and it will be discussed in a special event."

Zera looked at him. "Seriously?"

He grinned. "I know a winning subject when I hear one. Now, will you take more questions?"

"As long as they are not if I have all three of them with me at the same time."

Torun kissed her neck. "She does."

A woman raised her hand. "You mentioned the masks, but why do they all know you?"

"Torun and I were lovers beforehand, and he was my first patron. He knows what I look like. He has also recommended me to his team. They know what I look like. Because of my friend and fellow date being attacked, he is making the move to dox me to his fellow teams so that those who have thought fondly of me might keep an ear out if anyone tries to make a move."

He murmured against her neck, "Am I that transparent?"

She snorted. "Not hardly, but it seems that you have an agenda, and that is the only one I can think of."

She angled her head, and he nipped her before she remembered the audience.

A hand shot up, and the question was asked before she could acknowledge it. "What makes you different than someone genuinely beautiful? There are dozen of women here who have more allure."

Tycho answered that one. "You are un-activated, correct?"

The man frowned. "I don't understand what that has to do with it?"

"The activated sensory system is different. Now, for example, out of the first five rows, who is attracted to Zera? Be honest."

The folks in the first few rows blushed and raised their hands.

"Next five rows." The grins were easier, and hands went up. The rest of the auditorium raised their hands, male and female.

"So, whatever their activation is, they know that they can find comfort and solace in her arms. When Zera is with you, she is entirely yours, even if there are more than one of you. Everyone is equal, and everyone is welcome. But that is bought with trust. And her fees are extreme because the kind of security that the escorts need doesn't come cheap. Just the masks alone run into the high six figures, and there is one custom made for each escort."

Ryma hugged her and propped her head on Zera's shoulder. "She calls us her *little distractions*."

There was silence, and then, a woman with dark hair and darker eyes said, "How do you get ready for a date?"

"Um, it can rank from a shower and a change of clothing to a fairly thorough overhaul. It is all outlined on the initial date contract. Each encounter is a separate event, separate contract."

"What kind of thorough?"

"Waxing, shaving, enemas, lipstick in places you would not normally apply lipstick."

"Enemas?" The girl's eyes widened. "Why would you

43

need that?"

Zera looked at her and cocked her head. "Um, one of the prerequisites for this is that you enjoy sex already, with variety. As for why it would be needed . . . when it happens, you will know."

Hron was laughing his ass off, and Astel was snickering. Ryma grinned. "Don't look at me."

Naima just had her hand over her eyes as her shoulders shook.

She was suddenly between Torun and Tycho. There was an audible gasp from the folk in the audience. She pressed her hand to Torun's chest, and when he dipped his head, she leaned back, and the moment he slid one hand to her breast, she reared back and struck him across the jaw with her fist. The auditorium froze. She had just struck the most popular team member on the planet, and he had staggered back. His eyes were blazing as he straightened. "Pardon, Zera. I forgot where we were."

She put her hand on his cheek. "I know."

She stroked Tycho's hand wrapped around her waist. He had not tried to stop her.

The same dark-haired woman raised her hand. "So, you struck him and nothing? You aren't even getting a charge?"

"If it escaped your notice, I was being subjected to a mild assault. I also have more than a passing familiarity with the team member in question, and he was not going to stop once he made contact, and I was not going to stop him. So, it was best to stop it before it starts." She flexed her fist. "On the plus side, citizens, he is really fucking solid."

He lifted her hand to his lips. "Sorry."

"It's fine, but I have to work with these people who now not only know that I have sex for money but that I abuse my ex-boyfriend."

His eyes were hurt. "When did I become your ex?"

"I thought it was when I slept with forty-six of your team members. That does not scream commitment to me." She sighed. "And now we are discussing this in front of an auditorium."

He wrapped her in his arms, and Tycho addressed those gathered. "And now we get into the crux of being on the teams. You cannot have a normal romantic relationship. Any woman or man you can be in a relationship with is now a target for criminals, can be used to blackmail or extort your cooperation, and there is no guarantee that as your activation increases, they will be able to withstand it. You can't have sex with your teammates because it messes up the dynamic, and one of you is usually not really into the other. Your team is your family, and you don't fuck family. It is lonely, miserable, and you see the best and worst of the people around you. If you develop a craving that isn't socially acceptable, things get embarrassing, and yes, you will pay for folk like Zera to take you in their arms and tell you that to them, you are normal, desired, and cared for. It is intense after being alone for so long. Being on a team is rewarding, but being with a Blind Date is the best reward ever."

She smiled and did not tell the audience that Tycho liked to book her on the red days of her cycle if he was in town. Patron preferences were their business. Whatever it took to make them feel normal was normal.

The discussion came to a conclusion, all of the speakers were applauded, and Zera was pelted with questions about Blind Date Corporation by some of the other presenters. Her throat was sore, and her shoulders were tense as she was cornered and asked about services and rates. She told them all the same thing—contact management.

When she had a moment to herself, Alya came up to her. "Why didn't you tell me?"

"Um, there is a literal non-disclosure agreement. If Torun hadn't blown that out of the water, it would have been a shorter lecture."

Alya blushed. "I just sent my application into Blind Date.

Has management thought of going international with it? That way, there would be less stress on the local escorts and stop teams from clumping up."

"Um, talk to management if you get through the interviews. You are a business major, right?"

"Yes. When I talk to management, I will propose a plan."

"I think they will insist on you taking on a few dates before offering to make improvements."

"That is fine if I meet the criteria. I mean, I am good at my combat courses, but I don't think that I could strike someone."

"They live in a violent and physical world. A gentle touch is all we can offer, and sometimes that touch has to be wrapped in a fist."

Alya blinked. "That is really . . . accurate. Would you help me work out if I got an interview?"

"I would. Is there anything else you would like to know?" Zera smiled.

"How do you just have sex with multiple people? Where does everyone go? How do you know who goes where?" Alya had a shy expression.

"They decide that. You are there to react to what they need. If you feel like kissing, touching, or anything else, do it. Unless you are playing domination games. Then, give them what they are demanding."

"Wait. Games?"

Zera smiled. "No more unless you get the interview and sign the NDA."

"Well, can we go for coffee and discuss how long you have known Torun?"

"Oh. That. That is a story. And yeah, that is best told over coffee."

Alya linked arms with her and said, "Wait, do you need to say goodbye to anyone?"

"Nope. If they need to find me, they can. You don't even want to know how."

They walked to the coffee shop down the street and got the only table left at the front of the shop.

Their coffee was brought to them, and they sat there quietly before Alya asked, "So? How did you meet him?"

"I was at an apprenticeship conference in the capitol, and he was speaking. He asked me out to lunch, and someone tried to ram their car into the restaurant. He jumped in front of the vehicle and stopped it and then looked at me with this weird energy in his eyes. It took me a minute to realize he was horny, so I ran my hand up his chest and kissed him. It got a little more graphic from there. The first time wasn't comfortable, but it was intense. Things got more intense for a while, and then, he suggested sharing me with his team, and I needed a break. I took that break, and when Blind Date opened, I was their first escort. Torun came to me every time he was in town. I got my next client and was very nervous, but I just relaxed and tried to read beyond the briefing. It went smoothly, and he was so happy that he left a review for me on the team chat wall."

"Oh, wow. They do that?"

"Sure. They rate us while we rate them. It is all fair." She shrugged. "When you get back, you make a review of the client—failure to disclose details they require in the original request. Like, if someone said they wanted to take a walk by the beach, but what they needed was for you to tread water for forty-five minutes while they gave you oral from under the water. That is a very different requirement, and very different escorts would be offered."

"Shit. No kidding." Alya frowned. "I guess that it would be important to make sure that the client is matched to the escort."

"Critical. The mismatch I mentioned was because a serial killer had slipped through the cracks."

"What happened to him?"

Zera rubbed the back of her neck. "He didn't make it and was never seen again. It was recorded in the peacekeeper logs as a noise complaint, and that was that." She blushed. "The teams don't like it when someone breaks their toys."

"Oh, so Torun and the others . . ."

"No. By that time, I was seeing other clients. It was a different team that came for me. I was no longer strictly in the capitol. I had travelled when needed. I stopped travelling after that."

"I didn't know about that. I have known you for years."

"Remember those three months in second year when my voice was crap and I wore scarves?"

"Oh. Shit. That was then?"

"It was."

Alya blinked. "How long did it take you to get back in the saddle, so to speak?"

"Six weeks after the attack. I put a disclaimer on my file, and the team personnel understood. They handled me like porcelain for weeks until I grabbed one of my regulars and slammed him through the wall." She chuckled. "It wasn't just his eyes that got big that day."

"It seems pretty violent."

Zera sighed. "It is like having part of you that you always have to hide set free. The mask lets you do whatever you like, and there are no social consequences. If your patron isn't happy, you just don't get selected again. His or her review will let other team members know what you are like, so simply be yourself. All of yourself. The anonymity shields you and them. And, as no one knows who you are, you can make as much noise as you like."

Alya laughed. "That actually sounds nice. I saw there was a note about boyfriends or spouses. Isn't that illegal?"

"Under the activation occupation statutes, it is legal to restrict the employment to those who are not married or in a romantic relationship. Finding out that anyone has such a relationship is immediate dismissal."

"Why?"

"Stuff covered by the NDA, but it has to do with all that

48

testing."

"How long does it take to get a response back?"

"Up to three weeks. What is your activation?"

"Um, physical analytics. I have above-average reflexes and one and a half times my pre-activation strength."

"Good start. Have you accelerated any training?"

"No, but I am happy to if you will help me work out."

Zera chuckled. "I don't work out on site. I to go a private gym. Doing this as a side gig puts a lot of stress on the body, and if I could, I would get myself into one of those fancy places with a big ol' spa attached just for the massages. It is hard on the body. Don't get me wrong, it's like the burn after a hard workout, but it is rough."

Alya smiled. "So, you didn't say goodbye to the team today?"

"Nope. They already had me in the spotlight once today . . . and they are standing right behind me. Aren't they?"

Alya grinned. "Yeah, they are smiling at your back through the glass. Why does Ryma like you when you aren't into girls?"

"It is the contact she is after, not the specifics. They are missing touch, and sex is the socially acceptable means of touch for adults." She finished her coffee and slowly turned around. The team was standing and grinning at her. Torun beckoned for her to come outside, and the patrons of the coffee shop were all abuzz with the presence of the three beings outside the shop.

Zera sighed and grabbed her bag, stalking to the door and coming around to meet the trio. "What? What is it now? Foreplay in the car park?"

Ryma bit the tip of her index finger. "I think that's a great idea. That dress looks good on you."

"Sit. Stay. Beg." She glared at the team member.

Ryma moved toward her and stroked her hip and pulled her in tight. "Please. Please, oh please, oh please."

Ryma sniffed her neck and shoulder. "You smell amazing today."

"Um. Okay, this is unusual behaviour for you, Ryma." She ran her fingers through her companion's hair and pressed a kiss to the side of her head.

Ryma kissed her slowly, murmuring, "But you smell so good."

Zera kissed her for a minute until she leaned back. "Do you have something you wanted to say?"

"Oh, yeah, Torun had a thought. He thought you might become more of a target if we were seen with you. So, we are doing that now." Ryma cuddled close. "You just smell so good."

Tycho pulled Ryma away, and he lifted Zera against him. "I second the assessment of your scent. You smell amazing."

She held him as he nibbled and gnawed at her neck. When he actually bit her, she shuddered and felt one of her feet lifting slightly as she hung in his grip. He set her down, and he looked a little drunk. "You taste better than you smell, but let me confirm, lift your skirt."

"No. Be a good boy, say goodbye, and be on your way."

He grinned. "I am rarely a good boy."

"Ah, no, you are a *very* good boy." She pressed a hand to his chest and kissed him, tasting her blood in his mouth.

She was pulled away from Tycho, and Torun looped his hands around her hips, pulling her squarely against him. He leaned into her and inhaled. "They are right; you smell better than you did at the meeting. You smell like sex and sunshine."

She shivered as his lips grazed her ear.

He splayed his hands over her hips, and he chuckled. "Naughty girl, you aren't wearing panties."

"Everything was a little hot and swollen. The thought of anything touching me made me intensely uncomfortable. In this dress, no one would notice."

"I have noticed."

"Yes, but most folks don't have your vision."

"No, I noticed the way you walked. When you aren't wearing anything, you move with your thighs together. Afraid your honey will run down your thigh?"

"Something like that, also sudden drafts are surprising."

He chuckled. "So, what would you do if I lifted you up and took you here with fifty people watching?"

"Well, as I work around here, I would have to ban you from Blind Date for making me unable to work at my chosen job." She stroked his cheeks. "Do you think my scent could be caused by my other issue?"

He shook his head slowly. "No, this is all you."

"So, when you take your hands off my ass, you are going to leave?"

He nodded. "We have meetings in the capitol that we can't delay on. So, since they are all staring, shall we make it one for the ages?"

She looked at him and said, "This is going to be your way?"

He nodded and smiled. "It is."

"Here in front of everybody?"

He grinned. "They need to see that we are individuals with needs." He slid one hand up her hip and glided it up her back until his hand cupped the back of her skull, and he slowly made a fist in her hair, pulling her head back until she was helpless. His whisper was soft. "Is this how you want it?"

"Yes, sir."

"I thought so." His kiss melted her, and she was suspended by his hand in her hair as he kissed her. Her back was arched, and her body hung from his grip. When he had made his point, he slowly returned her to her feet and stroked her hair smooth with his fingers. "I will be in touch."

She staggered. "Fine, but if I get fired for this, you are off the client list."

"You won't be. Our charter has been made clear to the administration. They are going to offer you autonomy to recruit within the program for qualified candidates."

She stroked the front of his suit. "I am going to have to look for a manager. I really hate that side of things. I think I was just having coffee with a candidate for it. Why did you guys really come out here?"

"If I exposed you earlier, it is time for us to show why you are so very needed and respected." He stroked her cheek and neck. "This will all even out."

"I hope so because, right now, I feel like I am trapped in a blender."

He smiled. "It isn't nice to threaten me with denial of services."

"It isn't nice that you slid your hand into my dress and haven't even noticed."

"Who says I didn't notice?" He thumbed her nipple.

She sighed. "Just go. I have to salvage what is left of my reputation."

He kissed her softly and lifted her against him.

Out of reflex, she pulled her knees up to either side of his hips. He smiled against her lips, and she curled against him until she pulled away with a sigh. "Well, that blew up in my face."

"No, but there is a limit to the things I will do with you in public."

She nipped his lower lip. "Coward."

He laughed and eased her to her feet. "You are a charming contradiction of emotion and sensuality."

"I know. Enjoy your time in the capitol."

He patted her on the backside, and the other two passed her, touching her cheek and arm. When the group left, she could breathe again.

She looked around and saw Alya. Her friend's mouth was hanging open. She walked back to the coffee shop and picked up another coffee. She looked at Alya. "If you want answers to those questions, we can walk and talk. I have to get back to my lab."

Alya scrambled off the chair, and they left to a thin whisper that rose to a roar. This was going to get worse before it got better.

# Chapter Six

"What the hell was that? They were looking at you like my mom's feline looks at fish."

Zera chuckled. "Apt analogy."

Alya blinked. "They were all so cocky, they just reached for you, and you went."

"Yeah. That is how it goes. We aren't dating. They are authority figures. I already punched Torun once today. I wasn't going to get off easy the second time."

"What would he have done?" Alya shivered.

"Public sex was not off the table. Torun likes to get his way. He's bossy. He also enjoys tying me up so I can't get leverage. He's not the only team member like that."

"Whoa. Okay. So, that is fine. What was Ryma doing?"

"Sniffing me. Apparently, I smell extremely good today."

"And you let Tycho bite you?" Alya muttered it while they headed back to the research building.

"I taste good, too. He's a blood drinker. You didn't think that he got it from stored blood, did you?" She sipped at her heavily sugared coffee.

"I . . . didn't think about it, I guess. Does that happen often?"

"Them grabbing me in public? No. This is a first."

Alya blushed as they headed up the steps. "What was that last kiss?"

"Imagine us naked and extrapolate. He likes to fuck standing up."

Alya covered her face. "Oh, gods. This is humiliating and so interesting. Thanks for being willing to talk about it."

"Speaking of talk, if you want to try your hand at being

54

an escort, you are going to have to know how to ask for what you want. So, if you don't know how you like to be touched, find out. If you know a fast way to cum, share that information. They want you to be pleased with them, so they have a chance at seeing you again."

She sent the interview letter to Alya while they walked. Being able to use her fingers while talking was another thing that made Zera popular.

They went through the facility and parted ways at the black sector. Zera headed back to Susa's side, and she sat and sighed while news reports of the shocking behaviour of the team members outside the coffee shop began to scroll through the feeds. "Oh, dear. They are getting into trouble. Yes, I know I shouldn't be upset, but folks were really shocked by Torun grabbing my hair like that."

The dominating kiss was what had upset them. It made them feel less safe to know that he had that kind of impulse under the polite and powerful surface. He and his team were being interviewed on the matter, with international news organizations lining up to talk to them. She checked her com. Hm. Cool. No one wanted to talk to her.

She chuckled. "Since my talk a few hours ago, we have sixteen new applicants. That means there might be two suitable candidates. That's exciting."

Susa's body remained calm, and it was time to take her for a walk. Zera sat her up and slid into her. She manifested her com unit through Susa's body and continued working her way through the applications, as she dismissed a few who were just after sex or notoriety. They received very polite letters that thanked the applicant and stated that their application would be held for two years in case there was a requirement for their particular skills.

She did send a message out to the existing escorts to warn them about the upcoming notoriety and share the situation since one of their members had been exposed if they knew of any friends or acquaintances who might be interested in trying the escort option. Folks with healing activations were drawn to it, so she had a lot of med students.

She got a response from the professor, who offered two names. She would test the waters using the script that they had designed together.

Zera wore Susa around for about forty-five minutes while walking around, stretching, and doing push-ups in the body to keep it limber. Susa wasn't using it anymore, but it still had to serve a purpose.

She had just finished her time in Susa when her com started to light up with date requests. Her stomach flipped. Her regulars were taking up every window she had for the next two weeks.

Hron wanted the pleasure of her company for three hours that evening. Astel wanted the next night. Naima wanted to meet her for coffee of all things. All were requesting that she left the mask inactive. They wanted to clearly remember a night with her.

She bit her lip. That wasn't part of the deal. She wondered how many times she was going to have to say no on these dates. She hated saying no.

Zera went back to her office and worked on some new energy theory ideas. First, she set her manufacturing unit to make a micro version of the mask tech that could be concealed in a pendant, and then, she started answering some of the queries from her secure server. While she was paid via research grant, she was paid for the production of her ideas, so she had enough projects to trickle out for a few months in order to keep her association with the program ongoing. She had promised Susa's parents that she would stay with it as long as she could. She was trying. The next two weeks were going to determine if she could manage it.

She checked the testing schedule, said good night to Susa, and trotted off to headquarters. Hron had booked a private room at a very upscale restaurant, and he liked her hair curled, so she had to get on that.

Her new necklace was ready, as were the earrings, which served the same function. She even had a bracelet created to act as an emergency com. All of them were keyed to her biometrics and energy signature.

She got dressed, piled her hair up in thick curls until it could be held in place with precisely three clips, and then she put on her jewellery and an evening gown in soft grey. Her makeup was smoky and subtle. It was funny that she had to remember how to do eyes. A cloak hid everything, and her transport indicated that it was five minutes out. She took her guard bot with her and headed down for her ride.

The process of getting from the base to the restaurant made her nervous. If Susa had been with her at the base, they would have joked about how she was exposing herself by using her face when others had to use their genitals.

There hadn't been any contact from Mentor or the doll maker, but it would be soon.

She steeled herself and got out of the transport, letting her guard bot remain at the entrance. The hostess took a look at her and inclined her head. "How may I help you, Miss?"

"Private room two."

The girl blinked and nodded, leading her down the hall and to the upper level where the private rooms were located. Zera had been here a few times. She raised just the hem of her cloak so that even the tips of her shoes were not visible. No one else here was paying for her time, so they could not see her.

The hostess stopped outside the door. Zera lifted her recognition icon from her cloak, and it glowed blue around the doorframe. "Thank you. You may go."

The hostess blinked. "I need to make sure that you are welcomed."

Zera smiled and inclined her head from the shadows of the cloak. "Go ask if I am welcome, then."

"He did not wish to be disturbed."

"But he told you he was expecting a guest. So, you do not wish to let me in. That is fine."

She tapped the icon twice. The door flew open, and Hron was standing there in his formal evening wear. He looked at the cringing hostess. "My guest has arrived, and you are delaying our time together."

The hostess flinched. "Yes, Master Hron. Please excuse me."

Hron stepped out and took Zera's hands, kissing her palms before pulling her into the private dining room.

He slid her cloak off her shoulders and folded it over his arm. "Ah, dearest Zera, you have no idea how happy I was to find you unengaged for this evening."

He led her by the hand into the room where a long, low table was surrounded by cushions. Zera smiled. "It is *Master* Hron now?"

He grinned and pulled her against him. "It sounded juvenile from her, but from you, I could definitely get used to hearing it."

She inclined her head. "Whatever you wish, Master."

He shuddered. "You smell amazing."

"So I have been told, Master."

He paused. "I think I would rather that you call me Hron. You are too much an equal for the other term to be other than patronizing."

She smiled and reached up to stroke his face. "Hron, I have missed being able to call you by your name."

His hips thrust against hers, and he grimaced. "Too bad dinner is required."

She grinned. "By the end of the date. It is not required now."

His eyes glowed with anticipation. "We can do things out of order?"

She slipped out of his grasp and unfastened his trousers. "There are no hard and fast rules outside the contract. And the contract says you invited me for sex and dinner; it did not specify the order."

She eased him out, and he thudded into her fingers. She wrapped her lips around him and drew him deep into her mouth. His hands flexed, and he stood still until she pulled back and whispered, "This would be easier if you were reclining."

He moved them both extremely fast, and she was draped across him, wearing nothing but her jewellery. He was naked as well. They were lying next to the table.

She giggled and gasped when he slid two fingers into her, arching her back at the touch. "I am relieved that your eyes reflect what I imagined you were feeling."

She looked at him and put her want and need into her gaze. When he stroked her, she showed him what his touch did to her, and he inhaled sharply. "I see now why Torun suggested this as a possibility for you. Your intellect is astonishing, but your sensuality is off the charts. You genuinely are looking at me like I am the only male on the planet."

She smiled. "Right now, for me, you are."

He smiled and stroked her cheek. "Then, I will make the most of it."

Their kiss was sweet with a slightly wild touch. He turned her to her back and moved down her body with slow drags of his tongue and sharp nips of his teeth. When he settled against her sex, she moaned, and her hips matched his rhythm thrust for thrust until she bucked against him, and he moved up, sliding into her with a deep plunge.

Her lids flickered as she adjusted, and he groaned when he was all the way inside her. He remained above her, and she looked up at him with flushed cheeks. His smile was slow. "How can you taste like heaven and feel like sin?"

She chuckled. "Just the way I am, I suppose. How can

you be a speedster and one of the slowest, most thorough fucks I have had?"

He grinned and started to move. "Just the way I am, I guess. I like to take my time."

She grinned. "Take all the time you need."

He laughed. "Oh, I will."

His pattern was delightfully predictable. Every time she came, he changed position. In an hour, she had been screwed on or over every surface in the room and had cum five times. There was a moment when she felt a flash of cool air, and then, he was inside her, pressing her up against the wall while holding her hips. When she gasped and shuddered, he slammed into her and let out a short shout.

He pressed against her back and held her to the wall, licking the sweat on her shoulder and up her neck.

"Dinner will be here in five minutes."

She nodded and caught her breath. He withdrew from her, and she dropped into his arms.

"Zera, are you all right?"

She snorted. "Yes, I just need to not be on my legs for a few minutes. You tuckered me out for now."

He looked disappointed. "I thought after dinner we could . . ."

"Oh, we can, but first, I just need to rest and have something to eat. I just remembered that I am running on some protein bars from this morning, and my body needs more."

He chuckled and wrapped her cloak around her while he suddenly appeared in his formal wear. She leaned against him when the servers came in, and she felt their stares while she looked up at Hron. He glanced down at her, and it looked like he grew taller, just having her entire attention on him.

Zera stroked his cheek, and when the servers departed, he chuckled.

"Thank you for that; if I wasn't hungry, I would slide into

you again."

She chuckled. "You would have to do it with me prone. No strength left right now."

He grinned. "I had better help you get sustenance."

He held her in his arms and handed her a fork. He held each plate up to her, and she took a bite. She mumbled, "When are you going to eat?"

"When you have what you want. You know how fast I can go."

She sighed. "Yeah, but it feels so good nice and slow."

He chuckled. "Try this one. My mom used to make something similar."

She took a forkful of shredded meat and sprouts. "It's good. Kinda salty."

"It's supposed to be. Take a forkful of the purple shredded stuff in the middle." He smiled.

She tried the purple stuff, and her eyes watered with the salty-sweet-spicy hit. "Oh, gods."

He laughed. "Now, both together."

She gathered the combination and took a cautious bite. "That's pretty good. Okay, that's really good."

He chuckled. "It is."

She grabbed another forkful before he put the plate down. She sighed. "It feels kinda bad to be mauling this food like this. It was so pretty before I got to it."

He snorted. "It was designed to be destroyed. That is what food is all about, fancy or not. Can you eat on your own, or do you need me to help?"

"I can manage on my own. But, you start at normal speed and let me know if something is particularly tasty." She levered herself onto the cushions and let the cloak slide aside to expose her thigh.

He smiled, and she leaned on one arm while taking small forkfuls off the dozen plates that he had ordered.

She bent one knee, and her cloak slid away. The low table didn't hide much, and Hron was looking down the line of her knee to her inner thigh.

He swallowed. "You are a lot more tonight."

"Oh, yeah. The mask had a restrictor in it, plus with me being blindfolded, I was able to mentally remain in the requested scenario. No mask means there is a little more me at the moment, and that is a little trampier than most folks are expecting."

"You used to actually date Torun?"

"Um, yes. If you can call it that."

Hron frowned. "What do you mean? He speaks of you in such glowing tones."

She took a bite of something that exploded in her mouth. She swallowed. "Well, you guys can't really date. You can have lovers if you can find one who can physically match you, but going out in public when you have a physical aspect to your activation is difficult. Girls would rush him on the street, and he would have to sign things and parts. It would take up the time he had available, and then, it would be a quick fuck, and he would have to leave. When we occasionally had more time, he let more of himself out."

Hron smiled. "How often did you punch him, and how? You don't look like you have a physical activation."

She set her fork down. "I don't. That is not what form my activation took."

He frowned. "Are you done?"

"Dinner? Yes. It's all yours."

He blurred around the room, and then, he paused in front of her. "Try this."

She opened her mouth, and he put a sweet on her tongue. She closed her mouth slowly and sucked his thumb as he pulled it out of her mouth. She bit down, and a sweetly fruity liquid ran out of the tiny piece. She groaned and closed her eyes. He kissed her, and she opened her eyes, draping her arms around his neck.

He lifted his head. "See? It's good."

She smiled. "Yes, it definitely was."

His hands stroked her back and around to her belly. "You are naked under this cloak."

"Oh, no. And in the hands of such a dashing team member. You wouldn't be the leader, would you? Those are always the most dangerous." She smiled. "I am all helpless and naked."

"Well, it is a bad thing for you that I am not on duty. Helping you is the last thing on my mind." He slid a hand between her thighs and released the clasp of her cloak. It fell back, and he moved on top of her. "You are helpless in my clutches."

Her eyes went wide, and she breathed heavily. "What are you going to do to me?"

"Whatever I want." He pinned her arms above her head and kissed her roughly, moving down to her neck, and then, his mouth took him lower.

She moaned, and he settled in between her thighs. She exhaled power as her senses wound tight. This was the moment when part of her activation came out to play. She loved powering up the teams; she just couldn't tell them that it was what she was doing.

She rode the waves of pleasure until she screamed softly. He slid up her body and rocked into her hard and fast until he groaned and pressed his forehead to hers.

She stroked his cheek, shoulders, and feathered kisses across his lips. He looked into her eyes and smiled. "That is what I was missing. Seeing the slightly dazed expression is worth it." He kissed her softly.

Zera blushed. "The jewellery I have on is going to blur some details, it is mostly for the cameras and security stations that I pass, but it will have an effect on you."

"Will I get to remember your eyes?"

"Probably, but you have seen them before."

He stroked her cheek. "Not like this. This is different."

She looked at him and saw something shining in his eyes. "Ah, Hron, you have strange taste."

He bent his head and licked her neck. "You taste amazing."

She groaned. "Don't start with the licking." Her ten-minute warning chime made her sigh. "I have to get dressed."

He smiled. "Take a breath."

She inhaled, and when she exhaled, she was standing on her feet with her dress on and Hron holding her in his arms.

This was the part she loved. The coming down after the contact high. They stood together until her chime rang, and she pulled her hood up, stroked his cheek, and walked out of the private room, activating her guard bot for when she reached the lobby.

When she reached the home base, she checked her com. "Holy shit." Her available schedule was filling up. Her regulars and some occasional clients were booking her three-week window. She swallowed. The news had run highlights from the meeting and the public speakers. *Uh oh.*

# Chapter Seven

Zera changed and headed back to her office. Her security camera at home showed that there were interested parties waiting for her to come or go. Some were reporters, and others had eerie leers on their faces. She just didn't want to deal with it.

Her body ached from her encounter with Hron, so she spent the remainder of the evening going through the applications for the corporation and actually came up with seven candidates out of the accumulated twenty-one.

She got a call and chuckled as she answered. "Hey, Torun."

"Zera, are you safe?"

"Yes. Why?"

"Your house has been blown up."

She sat up from her reclined position on her sofa. "What?" She checked her security cameras, and there was no signal. "Aw, fuck. All my stuff was there."

"But, you are safe. Where are you?"

She yawned. "Trying to get some sleep. In my office."

"You don't sound upset."

"I am not, really. I figured that this kind of thing would happen when you blew my cover, so to speak. There are a lot of folks that consider team members akin to gods. No one can sully them, and I have sullied the hell out of you."

He chuckled and then said, "I want you safe."

"I understand. I want to be safe, and I am. No one without section black clearance can get in here. Anyone trying to get in here will be recorded by seven different cameras every second."

"Perhaps I should have been clearer. I want you with me."

"That is unfortunate. I want me under a blanket on my couch right now. I will shop for a new house in the morning."

"How can you be so calm about this?"

"Look, Torun, I am on very little food and sleep. I have work and a client tomorrow. I need to rest, and tomorrow, I need to shop."

"What aren't you saying?"

She sighed into the com. "All of my memorabilia is gone, as is Susa's. The bots packed everything after the search teams left. It was a preprogrammed response. All we lost was the shell."

He was silent. "So, you have gained some precognition."

"Logical extrapolation. Why did you strip my protections from me?"

"It was time. You are powerful enough now to keep yourself protected, and Mentor was not going to step out of the shadows until you looked frightening and exotic. He can still book you. Has he?"

She laughed. "The teams have fully booked the next two weeks. I would have to start booking two on the same day too, and I do have a job."

He chuckled. "Which pays better?"

"That isn't the point. Money is not the problem. The device design is so much more satisfying mentally, if not physically."

His voice came through the hall as well as the com. "Are you sure it is more satisfying?" Torun walked into her office.

"You know, I am going to look into your security clearance being revoked."

He grinned. "Good luck with that. You look tired."

"What did I just tell you?" She huffed and disconnected the com. "I am tired."

He walked to the couch, lifted her, and settled her against him. "Stop working and sleep."

She snorted and leaned against his shoulder. "You are not the boss of me."

He chuckled. "You are the scrappiest female I have run across with your soft side running wild when it has to." He sighed. "I miss you."

"You were the one who said that my ravenous activation could be fed this way. You were right, but it takes a toll."

He grumbled. "On me as well. I want nothing more than to come home to you and you alone, but I understand. Do you think you will need to do it much longer?"

Zera chuckled softly. "Until I can get more escorts to fill the emotional needs of the teams. You guys are messed up."

He pressed a kiss to her forehead. "We are. You are helping, as are your other escorts."

"I know. I watch your stats. You are pretty tough for someone who has the colouration of a flower."

"And you are pretty tough for a pain in my ass." He murmured against her temple.

"Ah, you love it."

"Yes, I do love you." He sighed softly as he cuddled her. "Now, get some sleep."

She tried to relax while her heart was thudding hard in her chest.

He lifted his head. "What is the problem?"

"You haven't said that before."

"But, you knew."

"I suspected. I hoped. I didn't know." She looked up at him. "It is nice to know."

He looked at her expectantly, his jaw flexing. "You feel the same, right?"

She chuckled and stroked his cheek dreamily. "Yes, purple pretty; I love you, too."

He looked at her in surprise. "How old are you?"

She blinked at the question. "I am twenty-four. Why?"

"I once met a girl who called me that, but it was years ago, and I was just entering the program."

She yawned and leaned against him. "What did she look like?"

"She was with a bunch of other kids, and her skin was translucent, her eyes wide and bright green. They were part of a find that the teams had discovered at a northern base."

She mumbled. "A find? How did you meet the kids?"

She felt her body winding down to a resting state.

"We were taken to see them, and the little girl got out of the fencing that they had her in. She looked up at me and said, purple, pretty."

She chuckled. "You were pretty then; you are pretty now. Don't worry. The others of my clutch are dead. No one needs to worry."

She fell asleep and could feel the riot of his emotions through the rushing of his heartbeat. Served him right. He had interrupted her own peace of mind countless times.

Torun looked down at his love. *Holy hells.* If he was right, this was the same woman he had met when she was a child. He had been fourteen and only recently activated. His skin was as much of a sensitive point as his having moved away from his family and losing his last name. Fifteen percent of the population were activated, and his parents were not among them.

He had been hurting, feeling lost as they toured the detention facility where a batch of six creatures had been found at an abandoned northern research base. The strange, bald translucent girl had stared at him while the others she was in with fought using a variety of activations. Her green eyes had stared into his soul, and he had moved on when he was ushered along with the rest of the group. They were an unknown species, and there had been no one else alive at the base. How the children had survived was a mystery.

He had continued the tour, and when they were looking at the med centre, a tug at his tunic made him turn around. The little girl smiled. "Purple. Pretty."

She reached out to take his hand, and a tremendous wave of power ran through him, but he kept control of it.

"Who are you, little girl? What are you called?"

She smiled happily. "Zero."

Alarms went off, and she got an upset look in her eyes. He knelt, and she threw her arms around his neck, hiding against him.

A female researcher ran into the room and halted. "Sir, you need to let her go."

"I know. Zero doesn't like the alarms."

The researcher blinked. "Zero? Right. Just a moment." She talked into her com, and the alarms stopped.

The little girl nodded and leaned back to talk to Torun. "Thank you. I don't like things that hurt my ears."

The researcher gasped, and Torun stood with the child in his arms.

The group with Torun was very still. It was obvious that the little girl was considered dangerous.

"Sir, can you bring her this way?"

Torun nodded. "Sure."

The researcher murmured, "What is your designation, sir?"

"Cadet Torun."

"Well, Cadet. We don't know what . . . uh . . . Zero is. We don't know what the others she is with are. But, the boys appear to be burning themselves out. They grow weaker every day. She is a little weaker, but she is stable."

"Why are you telling me this?"

"Um, because she is mildly radioactive, and you are the first person she has sought contact with."

He smiled. "I am radiation-resistant. It comes with the

purple skin."

The researcher relaxed. "Well, that's good then. So, if you just put her down in her holding cell."

"Why is she in here and not with the others?"

"What?"

"When we saw them earlier, she was with them."

The researcher paused and was about to speak. Zero leaned over and patted the woman's belly. "Hello, baby."

The researcher jolted. "How did you know that?"

Zero smiled and showed serpentine fangs. "Best friends!" She shot her arms up in the air.

Torun laughed, and they set the little girl in front of a sealed door.

The researcher knelt. "Now, how did you open the door, Zero?"

The little girl giggled and ran toward the door at full tilt. She ran straight through it and then ran out again, her arms out like the wings on an aircraft.

She stood in front of Torun and looked up at him. "Will purple pretty play?"

The researcher shook her head. "He doesn't live here like you do. He can't come back and play."

Zero's eyes got watery, and tears ran down her cheeks. He crouched and said, "When you grow up, come and find me, and we will go out and get ice cream."

Zero paused. "What is ice cream?"

"Frozen cream and sugar with an egg-based stabilizer in a variety of flavours." The researcher filled it in.

She frowned and stuck out her hand. "Deal."

He took her tiny pale fingers in his own. "Deal. Will you go back into your room now?"

She wrinkled her nose. "I don't like people looking at me."

He laughed. "You need to be seen, Zero, for people to know you are there."

She sighed and walked over to the researcher, taking her

hand. The woman looked surprised, but she smiled. "I will try and find you a new room, Zero. Or at least some curtains."

The little girl beamed. "Can I have a tablet? I want to make things."

"We will get you a locked tablet. You can show us what you want to make, and if it is safe, we will send it to the CAM."

Zero chuckled and nodded. "I will go to my room now. Goodbye, purple pretty."

Torun stared as the little girl walked through the wall and sat on her bunk with her feet swinging. She started singing and light took shape, filling the room with butterflies and birds that kept her company.

The researcher smiled slightly. "Cadet, walk with me, please."

"I have already sealed the non-disclosure agreement for this facility."

"Um, no. That isn't what I am talking about. Did you feel anything when she touched you?"

They were walking toward the secure wing of the facility. "Um, yes. There was a jolt, and I felt . . . stronger? Enhanced senses are my activation, but this feels like extra."

"Can we run some scans on you every six months or so? We want to keep an eye on your progress and watch out for any unusual activations."

"I have mine. We only get one. Right?"

"The radiation she emits is similar to that of the activated. She might be triggering something else."

"Do you think it was dangerous?"

The researcher put her hand over her abdomen. "I hope not."

"Oh. Right. You are carrying?"

"Yeah. I guess that it is going to be a girl if they are going to be best friends." The researcher chuckled.

"Do you know why she is thriving and the others are fading?"

"It's classified, but she is soon going to be the only one of her kind, whatever she is."

They walked into a med centre, and he was introduced to the curious medics. "He had direct contact with the little girl. She would like to be addressed as Zero."

The room was still, and then, they exploded into action, goading Torun to the scanner and checking him up.

"Cadet Torun, you have had a five percent increase in muscle mass, your tendons have increased in tensile strength, and you are going to need mineral supplements because your bones are thickening."

Torun flexed his hands. "That is what it feels like. Like I am about to have a growth spurt."

He could feel the ache in his bones, and then, the injections started. After half an hour with the medics, he was released as long as he turned to the team trainers in his home city.

"You mean the program medics, right?"

The researcher shook her head. "No, the team trainers. If you can pass your exams, you are going to be fast-tracked into the teams. I hope you didn't want to be an accountant or construction worker."

Torun looked down at his hands. "No, I wanted to be in the teams. I just thought it would be eight years before I got there."

"It will still be a few years. We don't know if this is a boost, a long-acting effect, or something that will make you explode."

Torun blinked. "What has Zero done to others?"

The researcher smiled. "Nothing. We didn't even know she could speak until today. What was the first thing she said to you?"

He was embarrassed as everyone was staring. "Um, she liked my skin."

"Exact words, please."

"Purple. Pretty." He would have blushed if he could. "Then, she took my hand, and I felt the rush."

"Describe it."

They recorded the details, and he was interviewed for all interactions with Zero.

He was brought back to his tour group with an explanation that the little girl belonged to one of the researchers and had gotten lost and refused to leave him.

The others in his group teased him about being attractive to all ladies, no matter how young.

He had left the facility, and the tiny girl in her tiny uniform had been standing on the roof and waving at him until the shuttle he was in was out of range.

He had no doubt that she was safe and warm inside the moment he was gone.

Three years later, there was a violent explosion at the research facility. Everyone found themselves outside the buildings, safe and sound. Torun had read the report. There had been no sign of Zero. He had just been put on his first team and had been on the scene.

The wreckage was absolute; there was not one computer or one wall standing. The destruction went all five levels down.

He had gone to find one of the first researchers he had met, and the man was blinking in shock. "Where is subject Zero?"

The man blinked. "Who?"

The lack of knowledge was worrying. He asked a few more of the researchers, and none of them knew what he was talking about had erased Zero.

Fifteen years later, he helped a young woman near a program education centre out of wreckage near the campus. The moment her hand slid into his, he felt the same surge of energy. The woman had smiled at him, but her eyes were a soft hazel.

Torun's heart had thudded in his chest, but he had fallen back to etiquette training. "Would you like to join me for coffee?" He blinked. He was supposed to excuse himself and exit.

"I have just had coffee, plus this shop won't be rebuilt for months, but there is an ice cream place across the street." She smiled, and his heart pounded against his ribs.

He held her hand formally, and she moved through the rubble like a queen. His team was talking with others who saw the attack.

Over ice cream, he tried to do his job while watching the smooth column of her neck and the curls of her brown hair over her shoulder. "Did you see who did it?"

She snorted. "Yes." She brought a name, address, and image of a rupture class activation. "This is him. He blew up, knocked the car loose, and it crashed into the storefront. He had been dating Selatha, and she broke up with him. Rejection is not something he can deal with."

"Selatha is the counter person with the broken leg?"

"Yes. They had dated for a while before she broke it off. He didn't take it well." She smiled and finished her ice cream. "Well, you need to get back to work, and I have to get back to class." She got to her feet.

The door flew open, and a young woman who looked like candy floss darted toward them. Torun was on guard, but the woman ran toward his companion and slammed into her. "Zera! Oh, gods. I was so worried! I heard you were in the blast; I came right away."

Zera stood nearly a head taller than her friend. "Susara, manners. This is Torun. Torun, this is my best friend, Susara."

He blinked as he recognized the bright blue eyes of the researcher in this woman. Of course, it wasn't done to ask about family.

"Zera, was it?"

She nodded.

"May I get your number? I may have questions about the events that need answering."

She grinned. "I have given you everything. I am sure you will be fine."

Susara was between them, and she chirped out the digits. "She turns folks down constantly, but she does it so sweetly. Don't worry about it. Unless you try and get violent, there is always a second chance." Susara laughed. "And folks call me Suit Bait. I think Zera's issue is just that she avoids the teams like the plague."

Torun had looked at Zera and the woman he wanted cleared her throat. "I am certain you are very busy, sir."

The downward flick of her eyes, the honorific, they were all things he wanted from her, needed from her. He swallowed as he nodded, and they left him on his own. Outside of the shop, Susara held her hands up, and Zera slammed her hands to her friend's above both their heads. The similarity in the name, the feel of her touch, seventeen years later, she was eighteen years old when she had been four, to begin with. He didn't know what was going on here, but the researcher who had been pregnant might have the answers.

He looked down at the woman in his lap. The researcher—Susara's mother—had died, and there were no answers on that front.

Zera rolled toward him and put her hand on his chest. "Don't worry about it. I will explain it next week."

"Why next week?"

She huffed. "Susara's funeral. Next week Thursday."

"How do you know?"

"I scheduled it."

"She's not even dead yet."

She opened her eyes slowly, and they glittered. "She will be."

# Chapter Eight

She was tucked in on her couch and still wearing her wrap dress from the day before. She got up, stumbled down the hall to the bathroom before grabbing some scrubs and going to the showers.

Zera washed and put on some loose scrubs that she used when in training with some of her combat toys. It was always better to dress in something that didn't provide resistance when using energy weapons if you wanted to know what they would do when they hit a body. She pulled on some ballet slippers that she kept in her desk and fired up her large computer, starting shopping.

She ordered the basics—dresses for work, underwear, shoes, toiletries, and haircare items. With her schedule, trousers were going to be out of the question. A few skirt suits and blouses were also on the list. She ordered her funeral clothing, and her stomach rumbled. She was going to have to go up and get a meal unless . . .

A knock at her door brought her head up with a grin. Alya held up the bag and coffee cup. "Here you go. Sorry about your home."

"It continues an absolutely sucky week. Thank you. You are my hero." She grinned and batted her lashes.

"Can I have a seat?"

"Sure."

"So, I am getting my interview with Blind Date."

"Congratulations."

Alya looked at her. "Can I just do it now, management?"

Zera sighed. "Six years of obscurity, and in one week, everybody knows my business."

"I ran through your financials. It took a while, but I used the security-breaking programs in the financial department, and I found your work data."

Zera ate the muffin, swallowing before she said, "Okay, but lock the door. The assessment is hands-on."

"What?"

"I have to test your reflexes. Every escort has gone through it."

Alya got up and locked the door, clicking the obscuring field.

Zera finished her muffin, drank the coffee, and got to her feet. "First, the questions. What is your ideal relationship?"

Alya blinked. "Um, an equitable mix of partnerships. Love, lust, and making dinner together."

"I noticed you don't say monogamy."

"It isn't really... I mean, if there was a set of partners..."

Zera looked at her, analyzing her responses. "You have been in a poly situation?"

"Once. I didn't fit. It was a couple who invited me in, and it didn't feel right."

"How would you feel being invited into a team scenario? A lot of the time, they are using you as a surrogate for the one they can't have in their own team. You would need to understand that."

Zera made some notes. Her computer was watching Alya's bio signs and recording everything. "Do you prefer a specific gender?"

"Um, male?"

"Normal. Do you have an objection to tentacles?"

Alya's eyes went wide. "I might tense up the first time, but as long as the person in question is not abusive, I should be fine."

Zera nodded and made a note.

"Now, I am going to show you images of different actives, and I just want you to watch."

"Should I pick my preferences?"

"You can, but it doesn't matter. You will go where you are assigned, or you will be dropped from the roster. No match made will be forced, but the selection process will assure you that the persons involved will meet your parameters. Even group events will all come from those who are authorized compatible. Your clients will have to adhere to those regulations, or they get struck from the books."

"Group events?"

"Where there are multiple team members and multiple escorts."

"Oh. So, you?"

"Maybe. Maybe others. It is up to the patron. Keep looking at the images." Zera flicked a key, and the projections of the actives lost some clothing. Some were missing tops, some bottoms, and a few were fully naked.

"Do you enjoy giving oral?"

Alya shifted in the chair. "Um, it depends."

"Do you enjoy receiving it?"

"Again, it depends."

"In general, if your partner is skilled, do you enjoy receiving it?"

"Oh. Yeah."

"And if your partner is attentive and enthusiastic, do you enjoy giving it if you know it will be enjoyed . . . and you won't be left hanging."

"Oh. Definitely."

"Good. It is a helluva ice breaker to drop to your knees." Zera chuckled.

Vids of couples having sex started on the projector.

"What is your opinion of the accessibility of the following positions?"

Alya blinked, and her breath rushed out of her lungs as the view screen showed a female pinned against the wall while a male thrust upward into her. They were viewed through heat signature only, and some parts were hotter than others.

"Um, it looks like it would hurt the lady's back from friction but, otherwise, really hot."

The vid changed, she commented, changed again, and again.

Zera watched Alya's responses through the scan on her computer. She responded to sexual situations with actual arousal, so that was something.

"Pick a scenario to watch, and get yourself off."

Alya blinked. "What?"

"Public performance is often requested. If you can't do it in front of me in a private office when I don't care, you won't be able to manage it with two team members glaring at you with hot eyes because they have bet on how long it will take for you to make yourself shudder."

Alya locked up for a moment, and then, she muttered, "I . . . er . . . the threesome. Two guys and a girl."

"Good. Do you want audio?"

"Oh, uh, yeah. That would be helpful."

Zera brought up the vid and allowed the audio. No faces or bodies were visible, but when the voices came into the mix, it was obvious that it was her, Torun, and Tycho.

Alya glanced at her, and Zera kept her hands busy on her terminal, running her answers to the questions, cross-matching, and getting an outline of acceptable patrons. She had a fairly wide net.

A training program was created for Alya, and as she sat in the chair with her hand up her skirt and the other on her breast, her head thrown back, Zera smiled. If she passed the physical, she would be five weeks from her first connection, and after that, maybe she would take on managerial duties once she had gone through most of the menu options.

Alya made the cutest little squeak and a low moan as she came; Zera put the audio cue into her file. The sounds of a genuine orgasm were in the escort files. It helped the patrons know what to listen for.

Alya sat up, dazed, and Zera closed the projection file.

"That was you, right?"

"Correct."

"How long did you do that?"

"Thirty-seven minutes. It was part of an extended session." She quirked her lips. "That was a long night and a sore morning."

"Did they hurt you?"

"No. My body just registered a protest. Now, Dr. Miliken is on the way, tidy up, and clean your hand."

Alya had sucked her fingers clean and just finished tidying up when there was a knock at the door. Zera opened the door from her desk's remote and opened the opacity. She sniffled, and Alya looked at her in surprise when tears were running down her cheeks.

Dr. Miliken paused. "Oh, Zera. I am so sorry. You know, I forget. You seem so business as usual until I look in your eyes, and then ... We need you in the development lab. What are you wearing?"

Zera got to her feet. "My house burned down last night. I am just having the worst week. No clean clothing, so I am waiting on some deliveries."

"Did you leave a note at the front?"

"Of course. Rehano has the information."

"Good. Well, can you come?"

Zera nodded. "Thanks for the chat, Alya. I sent you a message with the rest of the information."

Alya smiled. "Right. Thanks for answering my questions."

Zera locked her office computer from her wristband and followed Dr. Miliken down the hall and to the development lab.

There was something off about the doc today, so Zera kept an eye on him.

Dr. Miliken paused outside the lab. "Can you open the door? I seem to have forgotten my pass."

"Doc, it's in your wristband."

Dr. Miliken turned to look at her. Zera stepped back and yelled, "Security!"

Bots emerged from the walls and surrounded them. Zera dropped to her knees with her hands on her head. The bots verified her and turned on Dr. Miliken. The man backed against the wall and put his hands out. When he didn't use the specific protocol, they started zapping. He looked really surprised.

"Ah!"

The shot to the groin made her wince, but she remained on her knees until the security officers arrived, verified her identity, and then, they walked over to the smouldering heap of something that had been masquerading as Dr. Miliken.

She crouched and looked at the man on the ground. "Do I know you?"

"I held your wrists at one of Mentor's parties. He had me try to replicate you once." He coughed. "If he finds you, you are going to regret it. He wasn't gentle." He smiled. "He thought she was the one, but it's you. He wants you."

"Aw, I know. But, you found me, so how hard can it be? I think Mentor just isn't trying. I know he's not trying in bed, so he is just an underachiever." Her tone was low, and his eyes flared in outrage.

She chuckled. "Ah, so you are in there, after all, Mentor. Good to know. How many of your pets have you ridden around in?"

His eyes went blue-white. "A few. Several have even enjoyed your company, but you wouldn't know. You have those silly masks."

"They serve a purpose. I am guessing that they don't work on you."

"Not at my distance." He grinned. "I will see you again,

Zera."

The fake began seizing, and blood trickled out of his ears. The guards called for medical assistance.

Zera was shoved back, and she watched the man who had carried Mentor's mind into the black section of the program facility thrash around until he was still.

"That's nasty." She covered her mouth and stepped back.

She backed up against the wall and had a sinking feeling that things had just gotten very bad. They had been going so *splendidly* so far. She sighed, and she told the guards, "I will be in my office when they come to interview me."

"Yes, Researcher Zera."

She walked back to her office and sat at her desk, her head in her hands. He was a mind jumper. That explained so much. Damn it. Now she was going to have to rework her strategy. It also made her slightly confused as he should not have been jealous of Delvis. He should have just been able to take over Delvis's body and been the object of Susara's affections, but that wasn't what happened. She ended up dead. What had happened?

She lay with her head down on her desk. It was a fucking mess of a day.

The knock at her door brought her hand up. Her head stayed down. "Hey. How's it going?"

"Researcher Zera? We need to ask you a few questions."

She raised her head and looked at her guests.

Hron, Astel, and Naima were in the company of a mentalist. This was not going to be fun.

She looked at them and slowly straightened in her chair. "Come in. Have a seat. Sorry, I don't have more chairs, but I don't often get folks in here."

The mentalist looked at her and nodded. "I am the only one who will need a seat. The others are here to assure my safety."

"Excellent. You look a little on the frail side." He was

burly and six foot six easily.

He pulled the chair around her desk and held out his hands. She stared at them.

"Haven't you been scanned before?"

"Um, no."

"Extend your hands and look into my eyes. I will ask you questions, and my mind will touch yours. Are you prepared?"

"No."

"Good. I get better answers that way."

She extended her hands, and he gripped them.

She looked into his eyes, and he blinked slightly.

"You are not thinking about the events this morning."

"I am trying to think of nothing."

He nodded. "Right. State your name."

"Researcher Zera."

"What is your occupation?"

"Electronic weapons design."

"What is your hobby?"

"Escort."

He paused. "What?"

"I own and operate the Blind Date Corporation."

"Oh. Right. That's you. You look different than in your interview."

"I am lacking sleep, running on insufficient food, and my house burned down, so I am waiting on clothing delivery. And, I watched a man die. So, great day so far."

"Now, replay everything from just before he arrived until the end."

She looked at him and played him the memory, starting at shutting down the vid until the man died, and she hugged the wall as dread set in.

His thumbs caressed the back of her hands. He wasn't one of her clients. Mentalists tended to avoid contact. They saw too much.

"So, you know who is after you, and he admitted to

murdering student Susara."

"Yes. I had no idea that the man involved in her death was a body jumper; I just thought he was a pusher."

"In your other capacity, you believe that you have had sex with this man and that he confused you and Susa. Why would that be?"

"I don't know what criteria he was using, but Susa was Suit Bait, so I think he might have considered her more suited to whatever he had in mind. She was petite, delicate, and looked like she was made of spun sugar."

"And you are decidedly more robust for rough handling." There was definite heat in his eyes.

"Inappropriate, mentalist. Accurate but inappropriate." She blinked. "Is the interview concluded?"

"Not quite. Have you had sex with the teams around here?"

"Most of them, but until recently, it was only with the use of the masks that numbed the points of memory in the brain for both escort and patron."

"You had used this on every occasion before you were outed. Correct?"

"Um, there may have been the night before Torun spoke at the gathering." Her mind flicked through the touches, the hands, the heat, and the sounds as she remembered that night.

The mentalist exhaled slowly, his hands tight on hers. "That is certainly a bright memory. Anyone else since?"

She gave the memory of Hron to him.

"As the team is only here as security for me, there is no conflict of interest."

Astel exhaled slowly in relief, and Naima elbowed him.

The mentalist snorted. "Well, you are the possessor of a streak of bad luck and the target of a homicidal activated. I am recommending an around-the-clock guard with known guards. Ones that have mental resistance to tampering."

Hron nodded. "There are a few locally."

"If you give me a list, I can cross-reference it with my list."

Hron grinned. "You have a list?"

She shrugged.

The mentalist laughed, and she tried to extract her hands from his. He held her gently but firmly. "Do you have room on your roster for one more?"

She blinked. "You have to apply like everyone else. There will be months of waiting."

He smiled. "Of course."

"If you let go of my hand, I can give you a card." She blinked, and he continued to hold her. "Have you gotten what you need from me today?"

He slowly nodded. "You are cleared, and the investigation may continue."

"Then, come closer. I think you need something."

He leaned in, and she stood up slightly. He could see down her scrub top, and his eyes heated for a moment before she made contact with his lips. The kiss was sweet at first. His shock reverberated through him, and he adjusted to the contact. She heard a chuckle from Hron, a snicker from Astel, and a sigh from Naima. The mentalist continued to hold her hands, so she took the measure of his skills from the contact and flicked her tongue along the seam of his.

Mint tea was the first thing she tasted.

*"I drink it because I spend a lot of time face to face with suspects."*

She chuckled. *"If you can communicate this way, I am obviously not doing a good job."*

*"The kiss is excellent. I am just very nervous. Your mind has gone still."*

*"It is so you can just feel for a moment. Just feel."*

She leaned in and coaxed him into the kiss, and she felt his interest wake and flare, surging against hers. Zera continued the kiss until his body was tense and his skin was hot.

Her lips were bruised when she pulled back, and his chest was heaving. She smiled. "How was that?"

"Better but worse. So much worse." He chuckled. "How many weeks?"

"Mentalists get fast-tracked. You are under more security and checked more frequently."

A chime went off, and she looked at them. "I have somewhere I need to be."

Astel looked at her in shock. "You were almost kidnapped this morning."

"No. I wasn't. He was after some of my inventions. I have a lot of very small concealment and attack weaponry in the early stages of testing. Right now, the lab is an arsenal." Zera looked at the schedule. "I really have to go."

He frowned. "Why?"

"Invoking counsellor privacy."

He smiled. "Of course."

She showed him, and he jerked his hands back. *"Holy."*

"Now, now." She got to her feet.

He stood as well. "May I watch?"

She glanced at the other three team members, who were looking at her curiously. She shrugged. "You are all locked to secrecy if you come. Are we clear?"

They looked at each other curiously, and then, they nodded.

"Right. Come with me." She walked out of her office, down the stairs, cleared them into the secure section for a single visit only. Susara was lying still on the bed with her failing system displayed on the monitor. She was the ideal depiction of sleeping beauty.

# Chapter Nine

"**S**o, Susara wanted to try out for the teams, and to do that, she needs to go through testing. To do that, I have to do it for her and restrict myself to her capabilities and squeeze into her smaller frame." Zera moved around and unhooked Susara from life support. She checked the seals on her port sites and kissed her forehead.

Naima blinked. "You can shift shapes?"

"No. I am a jumper and nothing else." She removed her clothing and kicked off her shoes, setting Susa into a seated position. She scooted into her, and when she opened her eyes, they all looked different. The enhanced site that she had naturally wasn't in Susa's body.

She swung her legs off the bed and said, "Astel, can you grab me that student suit hanging on the wall?"

Astel brought it to her, and she put her feet into it, working it up her hips. She pulled her arms out of the smock and then slid them into the suit sleeves, working them up and fastening the closure.

"Susara?"

She looked at him. "No. She's not here. The only part of her that is left is this shell. This shell is going to the test prep, and tomorrow, I am taking her through the testing. She was far more than Suit Bait, and I want to prove that to them."

She looked at the stunned faces around her. "I will prove it to them. Now, I am going to go to the orientation, and you can do what you like. No one is trying to kill Susa . . . today."

Hron frowned. "I would rather that one of us is with

you."

Naima stepped forward. "I will go. We can get that coffee a day early."

She flexed her hands and sighed. "The body is pretty weak. I might need the help."

Naima offered her arm. Zera took it. "Gentlemen, if you would come with us. You are only authorized to be here if I am with you."

She herded them out of Susa's room and out of section black. She was leaning on Naima more than she was comfortable with.

"Sorry. I haven't done this before, so I forgot that I had to keep the body more active, including feeding."

Naima murmured, "If you can make it through the briefing, I will take you for lunch. It is common knowledge that Susa needs a guard, and I am definitely qualified."

Zera smiled. "You definitely are."

"Huh. Despite her status, I am not as drawn to her as I am to you right now. You are hiding your aura?"

"It is a chemical signature combined with energy output. It gets stronger the older I get." She chuckled. "And the more sex I have. I will have to retire eventually when I am no longer able to contain it."

She could see Hron looking back at her. "Retire?"

Susa-Zera chuckled. "Eventually. I am not going to leave anyone hanging."

The team's shoulders slumped in relief.

Susa-Zera chuckled, and then, they were in the bustling halls where students learning to control their activations stopped and stared. Susa-Zera grinned and said, "It is definitely you this time."

"I think it is us."

Hron turned and said, "We will meet you outside of the test briefing when you are done."

She smiled. "I will be fine. Naima and I are going to go for coffee before I have to prep for a date tonight."

Astel perked up. "We are still on?"

She nodded. "Though, you realize that folks listening in think you are going out with Susa."

He chuckled. "She is lovely as well."

Naima nodded. "We will be late. Out of the way, guys."

They walked together through the crowd and entered the auditorium. Susa remembered to log in, and the members of her testing class smiled and gave her encouraging words. She stuck close to Naima and sat in a seat surrounded by friends.

The order of testing was read out, and Zera sighed. She and Susa were only two people apart. That would give her a very tight turnaround to get out of Susa and into the right mood to keep her power in check. It was going to be tight.

Naima leaned in and murmured, "Aren't you going to be taking the same test?"

Susa-Zera nodded. "I have time, and I am automatically registered for the exam. Part of being involved in research." She kept her whisper low, and a few of the folks with enhanced hearing turned and smiled at her. Fortunately, Susa was registered as a research subject.

She watched as they were shown the procedure for the next day. They had their assigned times and were all going to be attached to a team when they entered and were given a briefing. They would get a specific task to accomplish, and they had to complete the scenario within the estimated time. Once the scenario was completed, they were free to go.

Susa-Zera had a lot to think about when she finished. Naima helped her up, and they slowly walked out of the building and across the way.

"So, Susa, what do you think?"

"I think it is going to be tight, but I can make it."

Naima whispered, "That is what I thought the first time I saw you."

Zera laughed, and it wasn't Susa's giggle.

"So, can you tell me anything about the actual test?" Zera asked it without being coy.

"Sure. Everything they just said was a lie. They are going to get you up and out an hour before or after your exam time, and you are going to be paired with some low-grade teams who don't want to be there or foreign ones who have a different way of doing things."

"Aw, shit."

"Yeah." Naima sighed. "I hope you make it to both calls."

"So do I."

They put in their orders and took a seat in the corner of the coffee shop.

"It feels so surreal. Here I am with both of you, but one of you isn't here."

"Yeah. Sorry. I know you liked her."

Their coffee showed up, and they sat together, thighs and shoulders touching.

"So, the body is dying?"

Zera nodded. "The announcement will be soon." Her voice broke.

Naima took her hand and held it.

"I am sorry I am wrecking our date."

"It's fine. It is nice to be able to be here for someone I care for, for a change. You have always been there when I needed you, and you gave me precisely what I wanted. It's good that you don't have the upper hand right now." Naima chuckled. "It gives me something to do."

"I am glad I could make myself useful." She smiled with watery eyes, and Naima kissed her. Kissed Susa. Someone got kissed.

When Naima leaned back, she smiled. "Your coffee has caramel in it."

"Yeah. You take yours black."

Susa-Zera blinked. "Are we on a normal date right now?"

Naima chuckled. "Of course not. That would be against the rules. We are here because your life is in danger. I kissed you because you needed it to remain balanced. And because you taste like candy."

Zera blushed. "That is Susa."

"No, it really isn't."

"People are staring."

"Well, you were nearly dead a few days ago."

"Oh, right."

"Have you ever been in me?" Naima ran her thumb along her knuckles.

"You mean like aside from sex?" She chuckled. "No. You would know, and I would have asked. I have only ever accidentally jumped in once, and it was only that first time. Incidentally, my body weight is added to yours, so you would really notice."

"Oh. So that is why you are having so much trouble walking."

"That and you are just so much fun to hold onto while I am short."

Naima laughed. "You are adorable and fun-sized right now."

Susa-Zera sighed forlornly. "I know."

Naima giggled. "You and your sister are very much alike."

"Yeah, we get that once people know us." Zera sighed. "Knew us."

"Did you want to get something to eat?"

"Sure. I have a date tonight, so I need to keep my strength up. Since Torun's little exposure of the corporation and myself, things have gotten busy. I only allow the bookings for the time I am not working, but since the incident the other day, all of my movie nights and dinners at home have been cancelled. My calendar automatically updated, and the bookings started."

"How does that work? I know with some others, it takes a day or two to get the confirmations, but you send it the same day."

"It is my project and my responsibility. Other escorts have jobs, nosy roommates, friends they have to attend to, and studying. Acknowledging that they have lives is why I have more signing up every day." She sighed. "For most, being with another activated person is a dream. To find one that matches them is heaven. I have wanted to set up a matchmaking spinoff, but since most of those matches are team members, it makes things awkward. We need a legal window so that they can have those matches with waivers for the municipal system in case the spouse, not on the team, is attacked. There has to be a rider or some kind of financial coverage for the neighborhoods. That is what the cities are afraid of. If the spouse becomes a target, who will be to blame. The teams worry that the spouses will be leverage, so they banned relationships, and other areas that employ activated personnel followed suit."

"You know a lot about it."

"It is literally a part-time job." She laughed.

"Well, let's go. There is a good place a few blocks away, and I can finally take you for a ride on my cycle."

They got up, and Naima helped her to the door and out to the sidewalk.

"I have to be downtown by six-thirty. Astel isn't tricky, but he is specific."

"Well, since I have to work with him, I guess keeping him happy is on the up and up."

The cycle came up and waited for Naima. She handed Susa-Zera a helmet and got on. Zera hadn't ridden behind someone in ages. She put her arms around Naima and held tight. In her helmet speaker, she heard, "This is a great date."

She laughed as Naima powered up, and they were off.

Naima took a number of sharp corners and accelerated quickly; it was obvious she enjoyed the grip around her. Zera slumped a little, and the fun was over. "Time to eat. I have had my fun."

They pulled up in front of a restaurant that specialized in noodles and spices. They were seated, and the food was out in under five minutes. The dozen condiment plates were fresh, bright, and went well with the noodles.

"Thanks for this place. I rarely get to go out for casual food. I do most of the cooking. Well, Zera does. Well, she will once we get a new place." She slurped up her noodles. "We might get a new place. Hell, I don't know what I am doing right now."

"You might want to get a neutral place. Somewhere with better security."

Zera chuckled and slurped then remembered she was Susa and changed her eating style to something daintier.

"Wow. You became another person there. Do you have practice doing that?"

"When Susa started with Blind Date, she was super nervous about dates. So, if the patron was physically enhanced, I would go along in her and help out during tense moments. It helped her get through the first dates. Once she had regulars, I could skip it, but for a few intimate moments, she would like me to drive."

Naima blinked. "With me?"

"With anyone. Once the first time was over and she was comfortable with the patron, she remembered how I did what I did, and the next time, their date was with her. I was like training wheels." She smiled. "I never did anything she wasn't a part of, but I made sure that she had a chance to do it on her own when she was rebooked."

Naima's eyes were wide. "That explained it. It was hot when you were with me but so much sweeter with her. Like she was a brook, and you are rapids."

Zera blushed and looked down. She finished her noodles, Susa-style.

"Thank you for the date, Patron. I suppose I should get a ride back to the research department before I have to head out."

"I thought you wanted a ride to downtown?"

Zera blushed. "I forgot what I was wearing."

"Oh. Okay. I will get you back there and then give you a lift to wherever you need to be."

"You don't have to."

"I know. If I get a call, I will have to leave you, but if not, I will take you to your destination."

"Thank you. I hope that some of my clothes show up, or I am going to be stuck in scrubs again."

Naima smiled. "I could find you something."

They got up and left the table, heading back to Naima's cycle. She took a direct route to the research building and helped Zera inside. Once Susa was back in her bed, Zera went around resetting her life support and gave her a nutrient bag instead of saline. They would need it tomorrow.

Naima blinked. "Uh, Zera. Your clothes?"

"Oh. Damn. Right." She put on the scrubs and her flats and headed back to her office with Naima on her heels. Boxes and bags were everywhere. "Oops. I shopped angry. Right." She went to one of her favourite manufacturer's labels and got a set of underwear and a different company for a wrap dress and a third for heels. "Um, do you mind if I dress here?"

Naima sat on her couch. "Be my guest, but make it slow."

"What time is it?"

"Five after six. I can have you downtown in six minutes."

Zera hit the lock and opacity screen on her office door. "Well, then, I have fifteen minutes to play."

"I am still on duty." Naima smiled. "But if you come over here, I can give you a hand."

Zera nodded, kicked off her shoes, and walked over to the other woman. "Where do you think I should start?" She set the bundle of clothing down next to Naima.

"Your shirt. Your shirt should definitely come off first."

Zera removed the scrub top, and Naima leaned forward

to flick each nipple in turn with her tongue.

"Apologies for being too tall."

Naima pulled her forward, her claws digging lightly into Zera's back. "No apologies necessary or desired."

Naima slid one hand into the scrub bottoms and murmured, "Oh, you are wet."

Zera chuckled. "Side effect of being cared for. It does not happen often."

They kissed, and the fingers against her moved faster until Zera shivered and clutched at Naima's shoulders. Her breath was fast, and the team member's eyes were shining. "Wow. The look in your eyes. Wow."

Zera kissed her softly. "What look?"

"Like I am the most important person in the universe right now. If this is how you first looked at Torun, I can understand him wanting to see it again."

Zera blushed. "Um. Right. I have to get changed."

"No one is stopping you." Naima leaned back and sucked on her fingers with her eyes half-closed.

Zera stripped out of the scrub bottoms, used them to clean up a little, and dropped them to one side. She wiggled into a pair of panties and put on a bra. The heels went on next, and the wraparound dress went on last. "I would like my transport downtown now, please."

"Folks are going to think I am playing the field. Susa before and you now."

Zera grinned. "Nothing wrong with that."

Naima got to her feet, and they were close to similar heights, but Zera had heels on. "You are majestic as all fuck."

Zera laughed. "You say the sweetest things."

They walked out the door and out of section black. The skirt was a little trickier, but it got them a lot more attention as it flared up and ruffled back to expose both thighs to the hip.

"So, Zera, you basically have bare legs wrapped around

me."

"Yeah. Don't worry, I have had my shots." She chuckled. They took off, and Zera held on as they zipped through the streets. She gave Naima the crossroads that she wanted, and they glided through the streets and traffic to their destination. Team vehicles had priority signals, and Naima hadn't used one of them.

Zera pulled the helmet off with her eyes gleaming. "You meant that to last."

"I did. Got you here with a minute to spare."

Zera handed the helmet back and smiled. "Have a good night."

Naima kissed her hand. "You, too." She stowed the second helmet and roared off.

Zera headed inside to get ready for Astel. The corset that he preferred took some effort to get on. She was going to regret those noodles.

# Chapter Ten

Number Eleven was in and getting changed for her encounter at her station. Zera waved hello and asked, "Did you need any help with anything?"

"Um, no. But... I haven't gone on a date with this patron before, and he seems super keen about... you know." Eleven gestured toward her extremely well-endowed upper torso.

"Oh. Ohhh." Zera smiled. "I am sure it will be fine. Everything is declared in your file, and he will be expecting it. The lactation is not a surprise."

"No, but it is a stupid activation." She looked down at her breasts as if betrayed.

"Maybe it is just what he wants."

Eleven shivered. "That is what I am afraid of."

Eleven's dress wrapped faithfully around her waist and ribs, then softened into bands that could be moved out of the way to expose her breasts. It was a design created with the greatest care. Susa had outdone herself. Just the right sex appeal without being overt. Eleven just looked like a busty club singer.

"Any jewellery?"

She shook her head. "He said he would bring what was needed. I just needed me and the dress. I even think shoes were optional."

Eleven looked soft, but she had a history that could curdle milk. Emotionally she was steel and one of the most competent people that Zera had ever met, but her body betrayed her by being soft, curvy, and she couldn't stop lactating. It was her superpower. She took care of abandoned babies in hospitals and got them strong and healthy before they went on to their foster or adoptive parents. She was as desperate for touch as her patron was.

"So, what do you think about Blind Date being outed?"

Eleven sighed. "I think it would have happened eventually. Sorry that it was so sudden and public, Zera."

"I will get over it. Torun might not. I think I am going to be busy on his nights. Washing my hair or something."

"Oh. Wow. I would love to see that. Wait. Strike that. With the way he kissed you, he would not take avoidance lying down."

"Ah, but therein lies the dance." She laughed. "Oh. Shit. I have to get into a corset."

Eleven giggled. "I can help. I have a few minutes before I have to go."

"Where is he taking you?"

"Hotel Del."

"Nice. I am there as well. We can share a transport if you like."

Eleven looked relieved. "Oh. Thank you. I have only had two dates before this and none with this patron."

"He is even-tempered for the most part. You should be fine."

"For the most part? Wait, how do you know?"

"I am management. I vetted his credentials." She smiled as she pulled out the outfit she had prepped.

"Wait. So, you are the one who recruited me."

"Well, yes and no. Someone else suggested you, and when you panned out, I made contact."

She removed her dress and underwear, setting them aside for going home. The tiny thong went on first, then the layers of chiffon, and finally the corset. Sometimes he wanted her soft; other times, he wanted her hard, but he always wanted her waist and hips encased in something snug and reinforced.

"Would you like me to cinch you up?"

"Please. Tight as you can."

Eleven grinned and said, "Better hold onto something."

"If I had a credit for every time someone has said that in the last few years . . . oof!"

Eleven jerked on the laces with precision, and soon, Zera was standing with her waist the smallest it had ever been. "Did you get the space in the back closed?"

"I did. Smooth line. Good girl for taking it." She smoothed the clothing and straightened the lines of the layers.

"If I had a credit for—" They both laughed, and makeup was finalized, masks were applied, and they headed for the lift.

"What do you do if they want to see your face?" They were in the automated transport, and Eleven asked.

"Tell them no. It is not in the contract. If you want to do it at a later date, I am working on jewellery that will blur photography and digital recording. Your mask does that now, but I need to make the tech smaller."

"Oh. Right. You can do that?"

"That is my non-activation activation. The people who raised me were scientists, and I got to play with all their toys."

"Well, that explains a lot." Eleven held up the tiny charm with her number on it that tucked into her cloak when not in use. "I wondered how these worked."

"They get one when they become a patron. You get one when you become an escort. When you have a connecting assignment, they glow and open the doors between you. I thought it was a nice touch."

"It is. It takes some of the fear away about meeting strange men in hotel rooms." Eleven chuckled.

The transport stopped, and their bots exited with them. They passed through the lobby and entered the lift, and Eleven fussed with her cloak. Zera smiled as they rode ever upward. "You will be fine."

"What if he doesn't like me? It is a bit to deal with."

"He will. I am confident of it."

"Why? How can you be so sure?"

"Step one inch forward."

Eleven frowned but did as asked. The invisible imprint of a face was in her cleavage, and as she stared, it moved, and a long tongue dragged itself across the creamy skin. There was a rumble of infrasound that ran through the lift.

Zera watched as Eleven was lifted and bodily carried out the doors and down the hall. She appeared to be hovering at a strange angle, but her patron carried her the whole way. The elevator doors shut, and Zera got off at the next floor. She wished Eleven well. Salat was a hard man to deal with.

She held up her charm and walked into Astel's room and his arms. There was something to be said for knowing what you were getting into.


Once inside the room, he set her on her feet and removed her cloak. She curtsied deeply and bowed her head. "I am sorry if my words gave offense, Patron."

His voice was so low, she strained to hear it. "The only offense would be if your profile lied."

"Oh, you mean uh . . . that part was accurate."

He knelt in front of her and became visible. He was dressed in soft shadows. Even kneeling, his head was still even with her breasts. She swallowed.

He drew his tongue over the exposed cleavage. He peeled the fabric away from her left breast, and he licked her nipple. She felt the heaviness of her milk letting down, and when he sucked, she squirted. The other breast started to seep.

He looked up at her with coal-black eyes. "Precisely as advertised."

He wrapped an arm around her to carry her to the bed.

He got up with her in his arms, and when she was on the soft coverlet, he lay nearly on top of her and stroked his hand up her inner thigh while he returned to sucking and drinking. He shuddered as he moved to the other breast, and she whimpered when she felt his fingers slide inside her.

She swallowed and clapped a hand over her mouth to stifle the whimpers as his fingers slipped and slid inside and around her until he gently bit her nipple, and she came apart. Her head went back, her neck flexed, and her thighs shook as her body pulsed in search of a cock to milk. Her low cry was one of despair.

"Ah, such a lonely sound."

She was glad that her mask covered her eyes, but the tears still fell.

He went back to softly sucking at her as if she was his primary source of sustenance. He reached for her hand and placed it on the thick, wavy hair on his head. She threaded her fingers through his hair and held her to him. She felt the slow, deliberate rhythm of his sucking, and she felt the flex of his throat with her thumb. She shifted her legs as her arousal started again. It was the first time that she had gotten aroused while an adult was feeding from her. Normally, she got comments about being a cow, but this patron had his focus, and he wasn't letting anything jar it. If the erection pressed to her thigh was any indication, he wanted her. He was just settling in for the long haul.

Her patron had three and a half hours remaining, and he didn't appear to be in a hurry.

He lay with his head on her breast, toying with the other. "Do you ever run out?"

They still hadn't actually had sex, and she was a little nervous. "Um. No."

"You wet nurse children."

"Yes, but I also pump to keep things from getting

ridiculous."

"You smell like coconut oil."

She blushed. "It helps manage the skin expansion and contraction. Cracked nipples are no joke."

"Can you lick them?"

She put her hand over the mask. "Um, yes."

"You get that question a lot?"

"I do."

"Do you drink from yourself?"

"Only when I am thirsty, and I can't find a coffee shop."

He looked up at her and grinned. The translation through the mask was terrifying. There were a lot of sharp points to his teeth.

"How do you see through that?"

"It projects a thermal image with a sonar overlay. You are grey and blue." She touched his hair. "This is black."

He smiled. She brushed the back of her fingers against his lips. "Your teeth are silver."

"That sounds terrifying."

"How long until you are full again?" He nuzzled at her breasts.

"I have a constant supply but will be topped up in about thirty minutes."

He made a happy sound. "Good. Will you pump for me and again before you leave?"

"I didn't . . . I don't have any."

"I brought my own supplies." He chuckled. "Just in case."

She shivered. "Oh. Okay. It takes close to half an hour to pump."

She swallowed and asked the question that was on her mind. "Patron, why do you find this interesting? There are more normal women on the roster of Blind Date."

"I have had a request for someone like you in with the agency since they opened up. How long have you been listed?"

"Ah. I have been live for six weeks. The eight weeks of training I had to get through was intense. I was way too naïve going into this."

"Do you regret this?"

"No, it has just been a lot to learn. Management doesn't want us to be caught by surprise when a patron requests something." She traced her fingers through his hair. His ears had a slight point. He had a physical and practical activation.

"You already know what I want. What do you want?"

She swallowed. "Patron, may I be frank?"

"Please."

"I want more."

He pressed a hand over her belly, and he smiled. "Explain in detail, Eleven."

"Um, I would like you inside me." She blushed. "More detail?"

He nodded. "As much as you can manage."

"Your cock inside me, your body over mine, and thrusting into me until I cum." She squeaked out. "If that is not on your agenda, that is fine, Patron."

He opened the side closure of her dress and started to pull it free of her body. "That sounds like an excellent plan. But, you have asked for it, so be careful what you wish for."

She got a little nervous. This booking had required a full cleanse with no specific reference to anal sex, and it was marked with a just-in-case tag. It meant that the patron wasn't opposed to wanting it.

She was stripped to her G-string in under a minute, and then that was whisked away. It didn't go with her dress; it ended up near a pack she could make out on a bedside table.

He stripped off the shadowy clothing and returned to her. His clothing had hidden elegant detail and a lot of muscle. There was also something going on below the waist that her mask was struggling to pull out of the shadow. It was hot, but that was about it.

"Now, you did not request foreplay, but considering the pleasure I have already had, it is only fair."

"P-pleasure?"

"My activation has made it difficult for me to achieve release. Milk from humans is one of the only means by which I can seek pleasure. Whatever gods have activated our secondary biology has a cruel sense of humour."

"Oh. Geez."

He laughed. "And then you appeared on my screen, and I was in town in time to make a booking."

She was blushing and knew it was not confined to her face. "I work a lot and don't check my messages often."

He started at her ankles and kissed and licked his way up her body. "How well does being a wetnurse pay?"

"It doesn't. It is my volunteer job. My day job is working in data entry." Her words tumbled out fast as her arousal started rising rapidly.

"Close to the hospital, I imagine."

"Um, yeah. I have a dispensation to take my breaks at the hospital and work overtime." She covered her mouth as his tongue move up her slit. The wet honey had started to emerge the moment he pressed his tongue to her ankle.

"That must be a lot of hours."

She mumbled. "We aren't supposed to be talking about this."

He laughed against her sex. "You are easy to question."

She shook as his laugh got her close to the edge.

Eleven gasped when he slid his fingers inside and crooked them upward, moving them along until he found something he was looking for. When he rubbed, it started as an itching feeling, then swelling, and then throbbing heat that built up with the feeling of his digits widening her. She nearly smothered herself in an attempt to stifle the scream that hit her as her entire universe wrapped around his fingers and the tongue on her clit.

He held her arched and tense with his fingertips sliding until she saw stars and slumped. He pulled his fingers from her. "Aw, poor Eleven. Can't take it?"

She caught her breath as her vision cleared. "Just. A. Little. Sensitive."

He chuckled. "So, you want me to continue?"

"Please. Whatever you do whets my appetite for more."

He sucked at each breast in long, drawing slurps, and then, he moved up and nuzzled her neck. "Are you sure?"

She knew there was something weird about his cock. She had seen that much through the mask. She sighed. "I am sure. If this is a one-time thing, it will be informative. If it were crippling, Management wouldn't have put us together."

He chuckled. "Very well."

She felt the blunt head of him pressing into her; he was wide, and she opened her thighs as far as she could to let him in. He slid in an inch, and she whimpered. He withdrew and slid in further. She panted, and he continued until he was pressed into her completely.

She panted, pushed at his arms, and tried to settle into a breathing rhythm that didn't sound like she was being crushed internally.

He sighed and feathered a kiss across her lips. "I did warn you."

"Move."

He paused. "What?"

"This isn't a parking area; either you fuck me, or you get out."

She could see the deviation in his colouring when she made her demand.

He chuckled. "Yes, Ma'am."

He withdrew and eased back, and her breathing got deeper, her body tightened around him, and she lifted her hips to take him deeper, even though she twinged a little. He began to move inside her in earnest, thrusting hard, and there was a tension in him. He was watching for something. He moved a hand between them and stroked her clit while thrusting deep, and she gasped and shuddered as her body spasmed around him again. She moaned softly as her body relaxed, and he thrust deep and held himself to the hilt as he spasmed inside her. She was so tight around him she could feel every vein, every twitch. His roar as he came made her ears ring.

Eleven gasped and flushed as his chest on hers caused her breasts to seep again. "Sorry."

He kissed her, carefully moving his mouth over hers. "That . . . isn't something I get to experience often."

"What is?"

"Being balls deep in someone. Is there by any chance another aspect to your active status?" His gravelly tone was polite, but his cock was hardening again.

"Oh, the hormones that cause the constant lactation also tend to keep my uterus and vagina very pliable. It does not come up in conversation." She winced. "It appears normal until pressure is applied. Then, it stretches slowly. My gyno had a field day with it."

"It feels like a snug fist, wrapping without strangling." He shuddered and withdrew before sliding back in. "Oh, gods. I want to live here."

He started a long, slow fuck, and she didn't know where to put her hands. His skin felt velvety but hard. He kissed her. "What's the problem?"

"Where can I put my hands?"

He pulled them one at a time and put them around his ribs. "Hold, claw, pet, do your worst, Eleven."

She bit her lip, and when he thrust in, and she arched up, she used her short nails to let her rub up against him. Eleven locked her legs around his hips and pulled him deeper with every stroke.

Her hands moved up his shoulders, and she held him close as he moved with determined frenzy.

She came again while grinding up against him, and he followed immediately as if he had been waiting for her.

This time, his growl sounded against her temple. She held him to her and stroked his hair while he twitched softly inside her.

Eleven sighed when he raised his head, and she swallowed at the distorted view of his face through the mask. She checked the display. Two and a half hours to go.

Her breasts felt heavy, despite the mess that was all over her and him. His chest was slick, as was hers. "Um, if you wanted me to pump, now is a good time."

He nuzzled her cheek. "Excellent."

He remained on top of her.

"You are going to have to get out of me sometime. Wrap up tight. Don't catch cold." She stroked his hair.

He grinned, and his pointed teeth glowed on her screen. He eased out of her, and she closed her legs slowly when he went to his pack. She scooted to sit up, and he came to the bed with a pack.

"You are sterilized when you go out on nights like tonight?"

"Yes. We get an implant that activates when we have a date. That way, we aren't flooded with unnecessary stuff. When foreign DNA enters, the implant activates."

He nodded. "Good to know. This is a design I have been tinkering with, so if you will allow me?"

He cleaned her skin, and then, he settled the units over her nipples. The units were attached to long tubes.

"Ready?"

She grimaced and nodded. This was the part she hated, when she needed a milking machine.

He activated them, and there was a hum against her skin. A minimal amount of milk came out.

"Why aren't you letting down?"

She blushed. "Put your head near either breast in light contact."

He smiled and did as she said and then licked the upper curve of her right breast. A gush of milk ran down the plastic tubes on her body, and they started filling. He watched. "Wow."

"Do you have spare tubes?"

"Yes."

"You might want to get them ready."

It took less than five minutes to fill the right tube, and a replacement was attached. While she removed the left tube and sealed it, he took the filled tube and used a heat break to divide the tube into packets. In the twenty minutes it took her to finish pumping, he ended up with sixty packets of milk to chill.

"So, you take one of those a day?"

He smiled. "Or every two days. I space my supply out. I don't require it. It is just a way of feeling something I haven't felt in a while. You have set me up for a while."

She grimaced and removed the pumps. "Free gift with purchase."

Her patron laughed and set about cleaning his equipment. She got up and took her sticky self to the shower. When she returned, the maintenance bots were busy changing the sheets, so she took her towelled self and sat on the couch with her legs curled up. He was fussing over his treasure, and she was tired. She closed her eyes for a moment.

# Chapter Eleven

Dozing off was against the rules, but the last three hours had taken a lot out of Eleven. She had one hour left, and then she could head home, and enough money would be deposited into her account to support her for six months.

When her patron touched her leg, she jolted upright. "Apologies, Patron."

"It's fine. It has been a tiring evening for you. We still have an hour left, but the bed is clean, and we can cuddle a bit before you leave."

"You got everything on ice?"

"I did. Thank you." He picked her up and carried her to the bed. He dropped her towel and pulled the sheets back, tucking her in and crawling in after her. He scooted down and pressed his head to her abdomen, his lips against her skin. He wrapped his arms around her hips and held her. She stroked his hair, and he smiled against her skin.

He moved up her body when there was half an hour left, and he sucked at her slowly and carefully, stroking her clit in time to the nursing.

She gasped and shuddered silently every time he teased her to climax. When she got her ten-minute warning, she stroked his hair and his pointy ear. "I have to get dressed."

His hands clenched on her waist, and he sucked hard before lapping until he had cleared all drops from her nipple. "Fine." He sat up, and she caught a glance of his erection that the mask refused to read.

She remembered her training. *Just because they are aroused is no reason to extend your time. They are not your significant other or a partner. They pay for your company, and you don't want to blur that line.*

He helped her back into her dress, fastened it, and kissed each of her breasts farewell. She put her cloak back on, and she bowed to him. "It has been an honour to spend this time with you. Be well."

He pulled her to him and kissed her hard. "It has been illuminating, escort Eleven. Get home safe."

She nodded and walked out. Her guard bot stepped out with her, and she returned to the lift. Her transport was on the way, and she exited the hotel with the sensation of being watched. The bot led her to her transport, and she slid into it; her token gave it the address back to the hub.

She thought she saw an exhalation of breath against the outside of the transport, but nothing else happened as the small vehicle pulled away and headed into the night. Eleven got to the home base with relief and went up to the Blind Date secure floor and changed back into her normal grubby clothing. In the waiting area, Zera was sitting with a smile. "So, how was your date?"

"Good. Weird. But good." She rubbed the parts of her face that had been obscured by the mask. She braided her hair into a thick column and flicked it over her shoulder.

"Why weird?"

"Um, I actually had a good time, and I think he did, too."

Zera chuckled. "Do you think you have a regular?"

"Oh, no. Maybe six times a year. He won't need me again for sixty days at the earliest."

Zera frowned. "Why?"

"Because I expressed enough milk for him to keep the packs on ice for two months."

"Oh. Yeah, that wasn't really accounted for in the contract."

"It's fine. It was going to happen anyway. I am sure that I am the only spontaneous lactator on the books, so it would be a rider in my contract."

"I will have legal look into it."

"Thanks, but I don't see it being an issue. I don't see any harm in giving it away."

Zera sighed. "Give it away, and it loses value. If you don't value yourself, they will start to take it, and they can do it. This corporation was developed to keep people like you safe. People with good hearts and a need for money. Or folks who just like screwing but who have generous souls."

"Why is that so important?"

"I looked up your client. He qualifies as special needs. You fulfill those needs, and he will want more. In fact, he tried to get it. He got this address from the transport display, and he tried to enter the building a few minutes ago."

"Who is he?"

Zera looked at her with a grin. "You really want to know?"

"Yeah. He didn't have a team code."

"He wouldn't. He's the premier assassin of the Aksalla government. They send him out to murder terrorists and slaughter them without trial." Zera used her tablet to bring up the information, and she smiled. "Do you wanna see him?"

Eleven got nervous. "Um. No. I am pretty sure that I will know him if I see him again."

"Are you sure? He's really handsome. Just the kinda guy you would want to curl up with on a cold night."

"Um, that isn't what I am in this for. I am tired of going to bed hungry. I just want to get a few months ahead of my bills so I can go back to school. Today should get me mostly there."

"Good." Zera smiled. "Would you see him again?"

"Definitely, but I know it won't be for a while, so I am not holding my breath."

"Okay. I will make a note in your file. You did good. Have a nice night."

Eleven left the building with a surge of hope. Her com

pinged, and the money was in her account. It pinged again, and she sat on the sidewalk. An amount twice the first had been dropped in as a *performance bonus*.

She got into a transport, set it to take her home, and she cried.


Zera lifted her head. "Salat, you can be visible now."

From on top of one of her cabinets, a beautiful cat man appeared. "I want her."

"I know, but she is free to do as she wills. If you want her, you are going to have to convince her. For that, you will need another date."

He grunted and ran a hand through his hair. "I am going tomorrow. I have other assignments I need to attend to. I wish to give her some extra funds. May I do that?"

"Certainly. There are performance bonuses allowed."

Salat grimaced. "Can I send her things?"

"Of course. Send them here, and I will make sure she gets them."

"Thank you, Zera. Is it possible to make her exclusive to me?"

"No, but she is a very specific taste, so I do not think she will gain much attention. I will definitely keep the curiosity seekers away from her."

He smiled. "Thank you. She's exceptional. I would like her protected, but in her occupation, she has no opportunity to be sheltered."

Zera chuckled. "She told you about that?"

"Eleven cannot stand up to torture or even light foreplay with some interrogation." He grinned.

Zera snorted. "So, not a fan of the rules all the way around. Fair enough."

"What is her name?"

"Will you mug my computer system to get it?"

"If I have to. I need to know before I leave. What is her

name?"

Zera looked at his cold black eyes. "Khytten Danforth."

He laughed, his sharp teeth exposed. "Khytten? Yes, that suits her. Wait, if she is activated, why does she have a last name?"

"She insisted that her activation was stupid, and she was refusing to go into the program or give up her last name. She said the only thing the program could have done was teach her how to squirt milk at her enemies."

He grinned. "It would have worked for me. I would have been on my knees."

"Yes, but you are the only big cat I have met and definitely the only one she has met."

He sighed. "Hopefully, the space between us will dull the burn. Thank you for your help."

"No problem. I am just getting into the idea of matchmaking. You two would be my first match." Zera inclined her head. "Get out, Salat. I am going to increase my security."

He snorted. "Do as you like."

He got up and walked through the doors and out to the lift.

Zera snorted. Khytten was going to have her hands full with that one.

Zera headed back to her office with the two test uniforms hanging up on the wall. Hers had been custom-made. She had five hours to sleep, and she was wearing both Susa's coms and her own. It was going to be a very busy day.

At three in the morning, Zera's alert went off. She pulled on her suit, grabbed Susa's, and went to get her dressed. In the middle of the night, she had had a brainstorm. She was going to get into Susa and simply expand herself around her to her normal height. It would slow her down a bit, but since she was called first, she could possibly put Susa in the maintenance cupboard while she ran her test.

If she could move them together, it would help when the active part of the test began. She didn't have to get best in class; she just had to pass so that her application to the research teams could be considered.

Getting Susa into her bodysuit took precious minutes, and Zera realized that she could have just jumped into Susa's body and gotten dressed that way. She wasn't good on three hours' sleep.

With both her and Susa dressed, they ran to the testing grounds. The huge warehouse of a building studded with guards was waiting for her in the predawn. She skidded to a halt at registration.

"Researcher Zera reporting."

The registrar smiled. "Twelve minutes is not bad but could cost a life."

"Understood."

"Your team and assignment are inside." The hand gestured, and Zera winced. She wasn't going to have a chance to put Susa somewhere. This was going to suck.

She entered the space, and a city under siege was in front of her. The team members that stepped out of the grouping made her happy and irritated all at the same time.

Hron stepped up. "Researcher Zera, we need your assistance in locating a missing person." He showed her a familiar image.

"You have got to be fucking kidding me."

Naima frowned. "We do not joke about rescuing personnel. Torun has fallen somewhere in this mess, and we need to find him."

"Right. Well, we need to find the rubble that appeared at the moment that com contact was lost. Do you have a record of the collapses?"

Hron smiled. "We do. It is narrowed down to these three."

"Which was closest to non-combatants and which was in

a combat area?"

The combat area was in red. "He's in there."

They snorted and said, "If that is your choice."

They ran off into the rubble and found the spot where Torun was likely covered.

She looked to Naima. "I am running a little heavy. Can you help me?"

Naima blinked and nodded. "You want to be at your best when you try the next move."

They found a spot without cameras or scanners, and Susa was gently set on the ground before Zera looked at the pile. "I am going in. I would step back a bit. This could get messy."

Astel smiled. "I think I said that recently."

She flipped him the finger and walked up to the pile. Hron asked, "What are you going to do?"

"Hop."

She sank through the stone and found the prone body under the rubble. She slid into him and felt a chuckle in his psyche as she pulled his body around her and then used his strength to punch their way out of the rubble.

She staggered out of the pile and looked at Hron before she slowly fell out of Torun's body. She landed on her hands and knees, cutting her palm before she was able to get back to Susa's body. She staggered into her, overgrew her, and then forced herself to her feet.

Hron wrapped Torun's arm around his shoulders and asked, "You okay?"

"I am fine."

Astel frowned. "You are bleeding."

She looked down and huffed. "It's fine. I will heal."

Naima frowned, and they started hiking back to the starting point. The team was upset.

"Don't worry. I give hand jobs with my right, not my left."

Three sets of angry eyes glared at her, and one pair

looked at her through slitted lids.

She shrugged, and they returned to the entryway with their missing man. Applause broke out, and Torun straightened and walked up to her.

She looked at him with exhausted eyes. "Did you have fun pulling the building down on yourself?"

He grinned. "Like bubbles in a bubble bath. You used to like those."

"That was when I had a life outside studying and work. When I had you." She swayed.

Torun caught her. "Easy. You have passed with flying colours. You need to rest."

"I can't. Susa just got called for her exam, and I need to be there for her." She chuckled. "You are going to be here all day?"

"Yeah."

"I will see you later." She pressed her forehead to his.

He whispered, "Take some of my strength."

"No. It would be noticed. She's supposed to be sickly, and this is the last thing that I can do for her."

"Fine. Do it for Susara then come and find me."

She nodded and headed out of the warehouse. She exited, walked into a group of trees, and became Susa for the final time.

She straightened her shoulders and fluffed her hair out, stalking toward the warehouse and keeping steel in her spine. She signed in and stepped through the doorway. Her team came to her, and she smiled politely. "Zurad, Menfall, Tiyak. Pleased to meet you."

"Ah, the Suit Bait." Zurad sneered.

She sighed. "Ah, the flying twit."

Tiyak chuckled.

"We have to engage an attacker. You are coming with us."

Zurad grabbed her, and Menfall grabbed Tiyak. Together, they all rose high, and Zurad huffed and tried to keep himself up. He was carrying close to three hundred pounds of female, and he had not been counting on it.

They landed on a roof and faced the crackling energy of Torun. She didn't roll her eyes.

"What do I need to do?"

Tiyak leaned close to her. "Convince him to surrender."

*Aw. Shit.* "How about he just beats you a little? I am pretty sure that I can do that."

Torun grinned. "Come on, little kitten. You can do this. Use that activation of yours."

She growled at him and walked forward, using the allure that Susara had in her body and projecting it. She walked forward, step by step, and Torun's expression grew less focused. She used her hypersonic frequency. "Come on, you are feeling nice and relaxed. Everyone around you is friendly. All you want to do is go and have a beer with the guys and watch a game. If you surrender, I will set you up with my sister. Zera's tall. Pretty hot. Likes being tied up and controlled during sex. You like control, don't you? You want to hold her down and do all kinds of things to her. Maybe tie her up, maybe a light whipping. If you ask, she would give in. She loves to give in. She loves you. All you have to do is surrender so I can pass this test and Zera can be happy."

His knees wobbled. He whispered on the same frequency. "How long can I have with her?"

"Two days. She will give you two entire days of your choosing two weeks from now, and if you are busy, she will bump anyone off the schedule to get you in. Sound fair?"

She kept herself on slow approach, and when she was close enough, she moved slowly and slid her hands up his chest, pulling his head down to hers. Their kiss was intense, but his eyes widened. "Venom?"

"I can't just be a pretty face."

He thudded to his knees.

She turned to the team. "That is going to hold him for

forty seconds. If you have cuffs, I would say to use them now."

The three men sprang into action, and Torun was cuffed. The two fliers headed to the gate with him, and she and Tiyak slid down the exterior piping before sprinting toward the gate.

She staggered up an instant before Torun snapped the cuffs. He ruffled her hair. "Clever little minx." He pulled her toward him. "I am going to hold you to that date."

She chuckled. "Over my dead body."

Susa got her passing grade with honours for doing what no other team had yet. Brought Torun to his knees.

She staggered out and past the incoming students and walked back toward the research lab. She turned off the monitors, draped Susa's body over the bed, and went outside. She turned on the cameras and said, "Hey, Susa! How did the testing go? Susa! Susa!" She grabbed her sister in her arms and held her, rocking as the pain of loss ran through her.

The body was dead, but it had gone for its final ride. The test was done, and now, the hunt could begin.

# Chapter Twelve

After Susara's parents had died, both the girls had their own funerals arranged. They didn't want to leave those decisions to their grieving survivors.

The autopsy showed that Susara's body had suffered an aneurysm. Zera stood in the funeral home's lobby and selected a coffin for her. Susara would go into her family crypt.

Standing there in black, she made the choices that she had to make. Susara had chosen her colour scheme, music, and even written her own final letter to be read out.

She would be interred in two days.

Zera couldn't stand still. She paced while the undertaker walked off to check on the dress that Susa had picked out.

The door opened and closed, the bell chiming a whisper of sound. She poked her head out and stared as Torun came toward her, wearing a black shirt and trousers. He was dressed all normal, and it was for her.

He came into the room and held her. Just held her. "I am sorry that I wasn't here sooner, Zera."

"It's fine. This wasn't a surprise. I am just glad that I got her through the program."

"You did good. Is she really venomous?"

"Yeah, she makes designer toxins, but she has to kiss you to administer them. And guys think that the teeth are the most dangerous part of a blowjob." She spoke softly against his chest.

He chuckled, and when the undertaker came in, he paused. "Team Leader Torun. Please be welcome."

"I am here for her. Continue on as needed."

"Right. Ah, Ms. Zera, we have the dress, and it went on without any trouble. Would you like to see her again before the service?"

Zera nodded. "Yes, please. Is she ready?"

He nodded.

She pried herself off Torun's chest. "I will be back in a moment."

"I am coming with you." He wrapped an arm around her shoulders, and they walked to the prep room where Susa was cold and dressed in her favourite gauzy gown.

Zera pressed a kiss to her cold forehead. "I miss you so much, Dainty."

The soft pastel hair didn't move when she touched it. All signs of life were well and truly gone.

She stepped away, and they wheeled her off for storage until they put her in the coffin.

Zera felt Torun's arm come around her, and he led her back to the office. He turned her toward him for another hug, and she stood there with tears wrecking his shirt. She lifted her head and brushed her hand across his chest. "Sorry. Here you dress up in a favourite fantasy of mine, and I get you all wet."

He murmured, "Normally, I am the one getting you wet. Turnabout is fair play."

She let out a startled giggle and a hiccup.

"Would you like to go somewhere and eat? We can get pancakes." He pressed a kiss to her temple.

She swallowed and nodded. "I think that would be nice. There is a quiet place down the block."

"Let's not bother with quiet. I wanna go loud. If they don't like that I am seeing you, they can tell me to my face. Before we were lovers, we were friends, and I want to be there for my friend."

She smiled, finished paying for the added floral arrangements, and left the mortuary with her current best friend.

He wove his hand with hers, and they walked over to a local and popular pancake restaurant. They were quiet together until they were seated and coffee was on the way.

"Where are you staying?" He kept hold of her hands across the table.

"At the office. I am having trouble imagining a house without Susa in it."

"Yes, it is a horrible thing that your house burned."

She nodded. "Just a cumulation of a very bad week. If I was easy to break, that would have done it."

"Have they found out what started it?"

"They have a preliminary guess of electrical. I am never very cautious with my power supplies."

"Is insurance going to kick in?"

"Eventually. For now, I have to decide whether to build or just rent a place in a building somewhere."

He raised her fingers to his lips. "A home is definitely in order. I have a nice secure place in the country just a few minutes outside of town."

She narrowed her eyes at him. "Really? That is a little far for my purposes."

"I have an express transport. It makes up for the difference in distance."

"Good for you."

He kissed the inside of her palm. "You could live with me if you liked."

"You are really on your best behaviour, aren't you?" She chuckled. "I have known you for six years, and this is the first time you have invited me to your home."

"The timing has never been right, and you have never needed me."

She smiled softly. "I have always needed you."

Their pancakes arrived. She grinned. Torun had ordered for her, and the result was that three varieties of fruit were on top of her pancakes, covered with whipped cream. She did like them as more cake than anything else.

He asked her. "What do you do with your days when you are not studying or working?"

"When Susa… I mean… I used to go skating, rollerblading, driving recreational vehicles through the desert. I take crafting courses. Paint and go out for coffee with friends."

"You don't drink?"

"It isn't recommended for a lot of actives. I am one of those kinds. Physically applied energy likes to get freaky." She took a wedge of pancake and fruit and shoved it into her mouth to stop herself from talking. He was far too interested in what she was saying. That meant he was taking notes.

"What do you do when you are not saving citizens and holding up buildings?"

He grinned. "If I can get a booking, I am doing you."

"If not?"

"Working out. I work out, especially if I have seen you. I feel stronger."

She coughed and reached for her coffee. "Do you? How odd."

She sipped, and he was smiling at her. "You do something to us."

"Not everyone. Just the teams."

"What do you do?"

She shrugged. "I don't know. I think of it as honing. I use my energy to sharpen yours. Help with focus."

"Why didn't you tell me? Did you tell anyone else?"

"Oh, gods no. No, this was something that was going to be figured out, or it would never be figured out. You obviously know that something happened."

"They think it is just us having sex that is driving us higher, but it is you specifically."

She blushed. "There are one or two escorts that have a boosting effect, but they have a niche clientele."

"Like Salat. I have noticed the briefings that he was in

town."

Zera smiled. "Oh. Is he? I have heard that his appearance is rather striking."

Torun growled. "Suddenly, I feel like striking it."

She stuffed her face again and hid her laughter. She swallowed after a while. "So, while I can take dates, I can't talk nice about Salat's features?"

He shrugged. "My love for you is complex, and women's love for his face and body is legendary. Once they get beneath the suit, they change their minds."

"It isn't for the faint of heart. She dealt with it rather well. Very well. He asked if he could send her presents." She smiled. "She should have gotten the first one yesterday."

Khytten blinked as she got to the receptionist's desk. "You called me, Mary?"

"This came for you." Mary gestured to the large box on the desk.

"Oh. Um. Right. Thanks." Khytten picked up the box and returned to her cubicle.

She was just about at the end of her day and shrugged as she opened the box. "Ohmygod." She closed it and quickly taped it shut.

Another ten minutes of work, and she grabbed the box, put it in her crappy car, and looked at it on the passenger seat. She released the tape and opened the box again. Blushing furiously. A very high-end cream jar was there, as was a bundle of dark silk that looked like a nightgown and felt like sin. A note said *Next time, wear this and this.*

She shivered. He wanted a next time. Nice penmanship, too. She fanned herself with the card, and she caught his scent. Her stomach dropped like she was on a carnival ride. The same danger-excitement adrenaline had her heart pounding.

She got her car going and headed home. The hospital

had the evening feed doses, and she had a present to examine.

Her apartment was tiny, so it was easy to lock up and strip before opening the box and taking the jar of cream. It was hyper-hydrating and non-toxic. She smoothed the cream over a nipple, and her toes curled. Damn, that felt good. The tiny bit that she had went a long way. She slipped the gown on over her head and tied the ribbons on her side.

She looked at herself in the bathroom mirror, and she wanted to cry. She looked happy. There was a robe that went over the gown, and she slipped it on a moment before her world blew apart.

Torun looked at his com.

"What are you looking at?"

"There was an explosion last night that the peacekeepers thought was a gas leak. An examiner took a look this morning, and it has been upgraded to a kidnapping. I might have to leave you."

"Who was kidnapped?" Zera got a funny feeling in her stomach, and she brought up the stats on her escorts. Eleven was in distress. "Damn it. What do they want with her?"

Torun frowned. "What is it?"

"Eleven. They have taken Eleven."

She made a call and left a message. "Just for your reference. Eleven has been stolen, and her tracker is at the following coordinates. No demands have been made, and an explosion was used to camouflage the abduction." Zera rattled off the location and paused. "I can dispatch a team if ne—"

A low growl sounded. *"Don't bother. I will bring her home."*

The call disconnected.

Torun frowned. "What did you just do?"

She sipped at her coffee, tense and worried. "I just told Salat that his toy was in danger."

"Toy?"

"They have had one night together and have not really spoken. At this point, he wants her for her body, and she feels the same."

"She wants her body?"

"She wants his. Affection will come later. Right now, each has everything the other one wants. They have to find out if there is anything aside from that."

Zera finished her coffee and sat there, worried.

"And our date is over."

She chuckled. "It wasn't a date. I was arranging a funeral."

"Oh. Right."

She took his hand. "It's okay. I know how this works. I want to spend time with you, too."

"Right. Where can I take you?"

She felt the gleam enter her eyes. "Team headquarters? I want to have a look at their electronics."

"That would be against the rules."

She shrugged. "Fine. We can go to the program research centre, and I can use the monitoring equipment there."

"What are you going to monitor?"

Zera chuckled. "If my hunch is correct, a massacre. And hopefully, Salat doesn't miss it."

Torun perked up. "What? I thought Eleven was soft and helpless."

"By choice. Not too far under that kitten is a tiger. She just needs to be properly motivated." She sighed. "I hate that this happened to her, but I think she needs to rediscover her claws."

"She had them before?"

"She did. Instead of joining the program, she took peacekeeper training but stopped right before graduation. Her parents had been in an accident, and she had to leave town. She missed the final exam, and when she returned, the heart had gone out of her."

"Why?"

"Her family is dismissive of her activation. I think that had a lot to do with it."

"You seem remarkably calm about this."

"I am not, but there is nothing I can do, and they have taken her out of local jurisdiction. Your team could manage it, but it would generate a lot of press that she really doesn't need. She feels strongly enough about being unusual; she doesn't like attention being drawn to her."

"And we have to go under authorization, which would create a why, which would mean that her name would appear in the news reports."

"The *Milkmaid* isn't something she likes to see in print or hear about in the news."

"Ah. You think she can manage things?"

"I think if there is no one there she needs to worry about, she can do just about anything."

Khytten groaned and sat up. Her hands were shackled together, and she was on a cot. Her breasts ached, and she gritted her teeth against the persistent heaviness. Her beautiful new gown was filthy, torn, and smeared with blood. Her blood.

She felt so stupid. She shouldn't have tried the clothing on. It would probably be fine in a box, but with it on her, it had taken the majority of the hit. Her hair was still tight in a braid.

"Oh. The little cow is up." The man had dark hair and glowing white eyes. "I don't know why the precog told us to kill you, but I think I could have a lot more fun with you alive."

She looked at him impassively. "Fun is not something I have ever been accused of being. Where am I?"

"You are in our little hideaway. Don't worry. No one can find you here. We checked for a tracking device, and you are clear."

He stroked her neck down to her cleavage. She jerked away. "Ah. Don't fight it, little cow." She grimaced while he cupped her breast and squeezed. The spray of milk was annoying, but when he growled, "That is fun. Let's just fix those cuffs, and we can enjoy ourselves."

Khytten smiled. He had the key. He leaned forward. She slammed her hands up, and when he reeled back, she struck him in the skull with the manacles. Once he was down, she hit him repeatedly until his eyes were open and the white glow had drained from them, leaving sad brown eyes that dimmed.

She rifled through his pockets and found the key. He didn't have a weapon, but many actives didn't carry them. She unlocked her manacles and tucked her breasts back into the gown. If they were out, someone had been playing with them. She didn't fall out on her own when the bodice was made this well.

She walked to the doorway and sighed when she saw a guard approaching. She wrapped the chain from the manacle around her fist and waited until he had passed the door. He continued down the hall and made a left turn. She counted to ten and glanced out, seeing him turning and coming toward her. She stepped out and walked to him, running the last few steps before she jumped up and slammed her fist into his face. He turned his head and grinned after taking the hit; his arms caught her on her way to the floor.

"Surprising, little cow." He gripped her, squeezing her ribs until she saw spots. "Looks like we need to tie you tighter, little cow."

She pushed against him, but he kept holding her until things went dark.

They took her attempt at escape seriously. The next time she woke, she was shackled to a wall with her ankles connected as well. The fuckers had strapped breast pumps to her. She glanced down, and they had only gotten a few teaspoons. The fact that her lactation was mostly voluntary was a boon. She didn't want these assholes getting any kind of boost from her.

Her ribs were sore, and there was a stabbing pain as she inhaled. Great.

She smelled blood. She took a quick inventory. It wasn't hers. She also wasn't alone. There was someone in the room. The scent of blood got closer. She felt a stroke on her cheek, and there was a smell under the blood. Her eyes went wide. "Patron!"

He chuckled. "Hello, Eleven. I got a call that you were in trouble. Luckily, I was still in town."

She shivered. He was carefully stroking her neck. "Um, thank you for coming to get me."

"Oh, I am not in the business of rescues. I do accept ransoms, so what will you offer me to free you?"

She licked her lips. "What do you want?"

"Oh, that is a long and varied list. I see you got my gift."

She hung her head, and a fat tear made its way down her cheek. "They wrecked it."

She felt his lips on her cheek, and his tongue licked the tear.

"I can get you another. You liked it?"

"Yes. It's beautiful."

He chuckled. "It is just well-constructed fabric; you are what makes it come alive. Now, you are shackled here in place, and . . . wait. Is that someone else's blood on you?"

She blushed. "When I woke up, there was a man with white eyes. He tried to play with me, so I beat him to death."

The invisible suitor laughed. "Why should I not be surprised? Why aren't their pumps working?"

"I don't want them to. They aren't getting it."

He chuckled and shut the pumps off, removing the harness they had put on her.

"Can I offer you milk for my freedom?"

"You offer me something that I can take for myself? Decline."

She shivered as he nuzzled her breasts, and she felt the change. He knelt in front of her and started to suck. He wrapped his arms around her, and she winced at the stabbing pain in her ribs. When he tightened his grip, she cried out, and he stopped.

"What is wrong?"

Khytten shivered; his voice sounded all dark and sexy. "A constrictor caught me and knocked me out. I think I have a broken rib."

He muttered something hostile.

"Um, Patron, can you take some milk and then give it to me?"

"How much?"

"A mouthful should do."

He chuckled. "You will owe me for parting with it."

"Right. I will try and make it up to you. Please."

She put what she needed into it, and when he drew, she hoped that he didn't swallow. He came up and kissed her; the sweetness ran down her throat. She shuddered and focused. The throbbing pain receded, and her abrasions healed.

"Eleven, how are you doing that?"

"My milk is a building block. I can make it create whatever effect I like."

He stroked her breasts lightly. "What do you put into it for me?"

She blushed. "I wanted to make it tasty and satisfying."

"No addiction?"

"Um, no. I can't affect behaviour, just physiology and biology."

"You added something." He chuckled and licked at her. "What was it?"

"Stronger and faster."

He chuckled. "Not more stamina?"

"Um, no. That was fine. I just wanted to give you something since you were so kind to me."

"Kind?" His hands stroked her breasts. "I don't recall being kind."

"Well, you could have been the kind of asshole who shackles a woman to the ceiling and floor in a negligee. Or the kind that ransoms freedom while she has her tits out . . ."

He barked a laugh. "So, you are feeling better."

"Yeah, my milk does wonders. Can I offer you any other biological enhancements that you would like?"

He was behind her, kissing her neck while cupping her breasts. "No, I think I am good. I mean, a smaller penis might be nice and stop the complaints, but then, there is one woman who took me and asked for me to go harder."

"Sounds a bit freaky."

"Oh, she was, but I am delighted to be on the receiving end of her attentions."

She shivered. "Would you accept sex as ransom payment?"

"Hm . . . to collect, I would have to deliver you safely home."

"Just . . . wait. Why are you in here when there are a bunch of henchmen out there?"

He chuckled. "No, there aren't."

"Oh, that is what the blood is all about. Why are you still invisible?"

"I did not think that you would take to my appearance. My features can be unpleasant when I am working."

She swallowed. "So, you kill people a lot?"

"I can get into terrorist strongholds more easily than any other agent of Aksalla. That kind of skill costs."

"Oh." Of course, he would be a citizen of the most exclusive country on the continent. She couldn't even visit. It was impossible to get a visitor's visa; she had had to sneak in to attend to her parents and had gotten caught and ejected.

She laughed at herself.

"What was that laugh?"

"It was for a moment of fancy. You come from a very beautiful country."

His tone changed. "Have you been there?"

"Yes, years ago. I used my visa application and enjoyed the landscapes." It was true, as far as it went.

"You entered illegally, took care of your family after a crash, and were ejected with prejudice a month later." He kissed her neck again, his tongue drawing a pattern on the skin.

"So, to be clear, there is no other person alive here?"

"Just you and I." He stroked his hand down the front of her gown. "I am seriously considering your offer of rescue sex."

She shifted her legs, and she cleared her throat. "I do need you to do one more thing for me before that is a possibility."

"What?" His tone was politely curious."

"Remove the sex toys that they belted into me."

"You kept up this entire conversation so well." He moved his hand down a few inches and felt the belt. He chuckled. "Look at that."

He knelt at her feet and moved his hand up her leg to undo the belt.

He removed two huge dildos that made her wince when they came out. She groaned in relief.

"You could have spoken sooner."

"I have been able to ignore it, but if you want to have sex, I need a minute to recover."

He stood and said, "Your ankles are free."

The manacles fell off in chunks. She flexed her hands. "What about these?"

"They are fine where they are for now."

He pressed his body to hers. "You know, it was your friend Zera who tipped me off."

She could feel his erection against the silk. "How did she know?"

"Your kidnapping was determined by an examiner in the rubble of your apartment."

"Rubble?" Her shoulders slumped. "Right. They blew me up."

He whispered. "They did what?'

"They blew up my apartment with me in it, then came along, and were shocked to find me awake. I got a kick to the head and woke up here. Well, not here. In another room that probably has a dead guy in it." She looked toward where she thought his face was. "They said that they were supposed to kill me. A precog had ordered it. Fortunately, most folks might be revolted, but they still get horny when I am around. That was enough of a distraction."

"They targeted you?"

"Yes, and addressed me as *milkmaid* and *little cow*. I hate those names." She grimaced. "The moment they called me that, someone was going to die."

He laughed and then kissed her, and her aching shoulders got some relief when he lifted her against him. Suddenly, getting unshackled wasn't high on her list of priorities.

# Chapter Thirteen

You are sure you are no longer in pain." His tone was stern. She smiled at where she thought his face was. "I am sure. I feel fine."

"You agree that your clothing is ruined?"

She nodded.

"Good. I will buy you something else." There was the faintest whisper of sound, and the skirt whispered to the floor. She was only wearing about eight inches below her navel.

She felt his fingers between her thighs, and he lifted her higher. His mouth on her breast caused two things, a rush of milk and a rush of honey.

She felt the press of his teeth against her skin as he smiled. He switched to her other breast, and the response was the same. Her fingers clenched in the manacles. She wanted to hold him, but he shifted, and his cock was pressing into her using her own body weight to complete the connection.

"Ohmygod." She panted and wrapped her legs around his hips for support.

"I have been called many things before, but never a deity. Usually, I am mistaken for a demon." His tone was amused, but there was a dark undertone.

He leaned forward and scraped his teeth along her neck. She shuddered, and it caused her to contract around him.

"Oh, that is good. Do that again."

She gasped. "Do it yourself. I am all tied up."

His bite was firmer this time, and she bucked against him as her body tightened up.

She hissed. "Knock it off."

"Why? I think you liked that."

She huffed. "Are you going to let me go after we finish?"

"No, I never actually made that agreement."

"So, you are going to leave me here chained to the ceiling with cum dripping down my thighs?"

He bucked into her for a few hard strokes and then paused. "Oh, that was good. Where did you learn that?"

"We get training. Verbal visuals are part of it. I get off feeling sex; you get off on seeing it, which is probably good for me because, otherwise, I would be screwed."

He gripped her hips and started thrusting into her. "You are getting screwed regardless."

She got to the edge far too quickly. She gripped the chains and used them for balance. He was a little surprised when she lifted off with him, trapped with her legs around him.

"Whoa, what are you doing, Eleven?"

"I can't grab you, I can't grab sheets, I can't push against the wall, and I want to cum, so this is my only way of increasing muscle tension."

"Set me on my feet, and I will cut you loose."

She lowered him back to the ground and grunted when she was around him to the hilt.

Her hands were suddenly loose, and she wrapped her arms around him. "Thank you."

Her shoulders screamed, but he started moving again, and the pain and pleasure welded together, and she shrieked as her body clenched around his cock. He waited for her to relax a little, and then, he thrust into her twice before he shouted his release.

She held him tight, her forehead on his shoulder.

"You are holding onto me like I am the last man on earth."

She murmured the truth. "For me, you are the only man on earth. Everything else is a pale imitation."

He kissed her shoulder. "I feel the same."

"I really hope there is a security vid of this because it is going to be fucking hilarious."

"You curse a lot more than I imagined a wetnurse doing." He chuckled.

"The babies don't care if you say it with affection." She stroked his hair and felt better now that she could touch him. "Patron?"

"Yes, Eleven?"

"How long are we going to stay like this?"

"Until I no longer feel like I am in heaven. So... forever?"

"Impractical. I have about ten minutes until I pass out, so if we could just uncouple and you can leave me here, I will get myself out of here even if I have to walk."

He snorted. "You think you can survive the desert?"

"Yeah. Pretty sure. I go sand riding a few times a month. It's how I met Zera. She probably sought me out, but it all worked out in the end."

He gripped her hips and pulled out of her. He set her on her feet and held her until she was steady. "Down the hall to the right. Two lefts and a right. The keys to the transports are on the wall."

"Thanks. Are you hanging around?"

"Watching a woman in torn and shredded silk with my cum running down her thighs cross through a battlefield to steal a vehicle? Oh. Yeah. I am watching."

He laughed softly and ran his hands over her waist to her butt. "Run, little kitten. I will be right behind you."

She whirled and sprinted out the door. She hadn't lied when she said she only had ten minutes. It was now seven.

Her body clock was pretty easy to gauge. Between the explosion, the tension, the sex, and the relaxation, she was heading for the floor in six minutes.

Chunks of people were lying to the left and right. Whatever her patron used as his blades was very effective.

She got the feeling it was extended energy claws. Nothing else in her mind could have cut through the metal.

She got to the keys and grabbed a few, taking them outside and triggering the access protocols. She checked each of them and selected the one with the most fuel and a flat spot in back for her to crash when she needed to.

"What do you need the hatch for? You keep looking at it."

"Three minutes from now, I am going to crash. I will need to sleep, and I can do it better in a vehicle where I can crack the windows and rest."

"You are going to risk your safety like that?"

"I want to not be here anymore. I can't stay here. I don't want to be here." She cried and slumped down against the vehicle.

He picked her up and said, "I will take you home."

"No. You said you wouldn't."

"I have changed my mind. I have an idea of the price of your rescue."

"What do you want?" She shivered.

"I will tell you later."

"Why can't I know now?"

"Because it would freak you out." He pressed a kiss to her temple, and a vehicle appeared in front of them. It seemed everything around him was hidden.

She sat in the transport and ran her hands along the leather.

He reached past her, pulling a harness over her and carefully between her breasts. The neckline of her gown kept her sensitive skin away from the straps as he used it and the robe to guard her.

"Why are you hiding?"

"Because I don't want you to look at me with fear or anything else. I am covered in blood."

"Blood doesn't bother me. Can I drive your vehicle?" She was nodding as she fought to stay awake.

He chuckled. "Maybe later. Rest. I will get you somewhere safe."

"Okay. No groping while I am out."

He laughed. "No promises."

She chuckled as darkness swam up and wrapped around her. On to another part of her ordeal.

Khytten squirmed in the soft bedding, and she sighed. She had vague memories of a female voice and soft hands. Her aches and pains were gone. The full-body throb that had been driving her to distraction was gone.

"You were hiding things from me, Eleven. Internal injuries, concussion, fractured wrist, broken rib. You healed a little, but I think it would take far more than you were willing to consume in front of me to heal you."

She blinked and looked toward the shadows. There was a visible person there, but his face was in shadow. His body took her breath away, but she couldn't see the rest of him.

"Um, I have a very active endorphin-release system. I can move past the pain fairly easily. My body usually hurts in some way or another. It keeps me moving." She looked at the light. "Shit. I need to get to the hospital."

"No, you don't. You have expressed twice, and the milk has been delivered to the patients in your care."

She was naked between the sheets and held the top sheet to her chest as she sat up. "I . . . thank you."

"You are welcome. You needed rest, and the healer helped me, though she was slightly appalled that I knew how to trigger it."

Eleven ran her hand along her scalp. "Someone washed my hair?"

"I washed all of you. There was blood everywhere. The Mentor really did blow you up."

She frowned. "What? Why?"

"Because a precog told him that you were pivotal to what happened next."

"The guy who had me didn't tell me that."

"The men I questioned were more . . . forthcoming."

"Oh. Right." She blushed and looked around. "We aren't at a hotel."

"This is a place the Aksalla government keeps for my travels. They have similar places around the world."

She nodded. "Um, is there anything I can wear?"

"You are doing pretty well with that sheet."

The air caressed her back and hips. "I would like to leave the bed."

"Leave it; I am not stopping you."

She gave him a narrow-eyed look. "Don't you have people to kill or something?"

He laughed. "Usually. Today, my attention is all for you."

"That is remarkably un-reassuring."

"Good." He got up and went to a dresser. He pulled out a piece of fabric and brought it to her, dropping it in her lap. "Wear that."

She looked at the t-shirt that would swamp her. "This is yours."

"It's clean. You are safe."

She snorted and pulled the fabric over her head then slid her legs out of bed and tugged it down to mid-thigh. "Thanks."

"I will add it to your bill."

"Um, about that. What is my tally so far? I don't know if I can afford to ask for breakfast." She pulled her hair out of the shirt and started braiding it.

"Why do you do that?"

She grimaced. "Milk is sticky."

"Feel free to go exploring. I have to contact Zera and let her know you are awake. She was worried."

"Okay." She got up and bolted for the door.

She was out the door and down the hall in a few seconds, and then, a warm iron bar wrapped around her belly. "Where are you going, little prey?"

"Um, high-speed tour?"

He chuckled. "Not fast enough. You will have to work on your speed, Eleven."

She turned her head and blinked. "Um. I can see you."

"Yes. I don't hide in my own home."

"I thought you said it was a government building."

"It is, and it isn't. Now, where were you running to, Eleven?"

"Kitchen?"

"That eager for breakfast? Maybe I should help you."

He lifted her and carried her through the halls of the large home and into a bright and cheerful kitchen that did not match the man with black velvet skin, black eyes, and pointed ears. He was super handsome—high cheekbones, a sharp nose, and firm and pleasantly curved lips.

"You are staring."

"You are quite pretty."

He laughed. "So I have been told."

He set her down on the kitchen counter. "What can I get for you?"

She reached out to touch him but pulled her hand back. "Um. A muffin, toast, anything?"

"Breakfast in exchange for a kiss."

She blinked. "Ah. Okay, I guess. I haven't brushed my teeth."

He grinned. "I did."

"What?"

"I brushed your teeth, bathed you, brushed your hair, and dried it. It is super silky, by the way." He nipped her lower lip before he pressed inward for a kiss that left her breathless. "So, there, I have given you a kiss, now give one to me, and we will get you fed."

She blushed and put her hands on his shoulders, leaning in until she was making contact with his lips. She started the kiss slowly and deepened it. His hands clenched on her waist and flexed as she slid her tongue along his, past the sharp points of his teeth as she enjoyed the simple and basic contact with him, her nipples pressing against the inside of the shirt showed her that she was enjoying the touch on a basic level that had nothing to do with contracts, dates, or panic. She just enjoyed her patron as a man, and he reciprocated her appreciation.

When she lifted her head, her breathing was rapid. "And a cup of coffee."

He grinned. "I can manage that."

"I can get it myself, but there seems to be something stopping me from leaving the counter."

"Your feet are bare, and the floor is cold. You stay there, and I will fix your breakfast."

She blinked and nodded. "Okay."

He turned her to face inside the workspace of the kitchen, and he set the coffee up before he returned to her and eased her thighs apart a little. She blushed when he would pause and lick gently inside her knee, then her thigh, and her inner thigh.

He presented her with scrambled eggs, toast, and some fruit salad with her coffee next to her on the counter.

She picked up her coffee and sipped it. "I . . . Did you already eat?"

He smiled and leaned against the counter opposite her. "No. I had plenty to eat last night."

"Oh, uh. Right."

"So, you can really create designer reactions via your milk?"

"Yes. For babies, I give them strong immune systems and treatments to counteract anything noxious in their systems. I haven't fed many adults, so I do it on a case-by-case basis."

He nodded. "Eat your breakfast."

She ate, and he stared at her, getting more and more tense as she finished the last piece of fruit in the salad. Two swallows of coffee and the empty cup was set aside. "Thank you."

"You are very polite for someone who curses as much as you do."

She slowly started to close her thighs, and his gaze locked with hers.

"Stop."

She looked him over; his tight tank top and snug pants left little to the imagination. "I imagine that your family freaked out a little when you activated."

"Yeah. Not quite like yours did. My family was excited at the possibilities. I received developmental training, the most aggressive technological education available, and plenty of subversive training."

She swung her feet a little. "I got to go to active camp. That was a lawsuit that I won't forget."

"Your parents sued?"

She snorted. "No, the camp sued me for sexually harassing their counsellors."

"What?"

"Yeah. My parents had to emancipate me to stop me from taking them down with them; they changed their name and moved away."

"And where did they go?" He started to move toward her.

"I am guessing that you already know."

"Yes, but tell me."

"They went to Aksalla. They joined a research facility, and my sister has a coffee shop there. They got their permanent residence just before the lock was enacted."

"So, when your sister called for help, you came running."

"Yes. They are my family."

"They abandoned you for expedience." He stood between her thighs and rubbed at her knees. "That is not what family does."

She lifted her chin and stared into his all-black eyes. "It might not be what your family would do, but it was what mine did."

"And then your sister denied summoning you and left you to take the fall for your lack of proper registration."

"So, you know the story."

"I did some research. Your parents didn't accept your help?"

She looked down. "You mean that? No. They find the idea disgusting. They find me and my body disgusting and couldn't believe my sister had called for me. I got them back on their feet and put my milk in their coffee starting at week three. They got better, and by week five, they asked me to leave, and when I didn't do it quickly enough, they called the authorities."

"It was my sister that arrested you, by the way."

"Wonderful."

He kissed her softly. "I haven't asked her about her opinion of you, but her report regarding your family was scathing."

She sighed softly as his tongue taunted hers into moving with him. "Past is the past."

"And yet, it shapes who we are." He threaded a hand through her hair and held her as he brushed kisses across her forehead, eyelids, and the tip of her nose. "You are adorable."

She didn't know where to look. "Uh. Thank you."

"I don't think I have ever been thanked for stating the obvious before."

She kept her mouth shut.

"You are silent because you would argue with me? It is not wise to tell me that I am wrong."

"How about that you have a skewed perspective?" He smiled, and it was not a nice smile. She quickly added. "A unique perspective?"

"It is that. I see you because I am really looking." He drew his finger down the front of her shirt, and to her shock, the tee split an instant behind his fingertip.

"What is that?"

He grinned. "I am really looking, and I haven't had breakfast yet."

She blushed and yelped as he ran his tongue over her, and her particular talent overflowed.

She threaded her fingers through his hair and held him. He flicked his eyes toward her and met her gaze as he sucked.

Her voice was husky, and she whispered, "You wrecked your own shirt."

He released that nipple and laughed. "Worth it."

She flinched when he attached to the other side and swallowed while looking at her. He slid his fingers into her and thumbed her clit. He started with two and then added a third as his hand moved in time to the sucking.

Khytten felt herself tighten around his fingers, and his sucking involved grazes of his teeth. It took less than a dozen strokes before she moaned low and her muscles gripped his fingers. He continued to move his digits inside her while her body clasped and released him. She shuddered as he slowly sucked at her.

He licked at her breasts and said, "You taste different when you cum."

"I have never actually tested that."

"You don't need to. You taste like sex, but just until the spasms stop then it is all sweetness again. You program it as it exits."

She wrinkled her nose. "Why did I tell you all that?"

"Because I asked, and no one else has. You know all these wonderful things about your body and have no one to tell. It must be frustrating." He smiled. "I am genuinely interested in how your body works. Allow me to demonstrate."

He opened his trousers, the thick skin-tight fabric pressed on her inner thighs as he leaned in and pressed against her. Her body resisted for a moment, and then, she welcomed him in, gloving around him.

He shuddered. "Oh, that is good."

The rush of heat that moved through her was intense as he started to move. She gripped his neck with one hand and used the other to brace herself as she moved with him.

When he touched her, it seemed like the most logical thing in the world. When she looked in his eyes, he was everything that should terrify her and everything that didn't.

Khytten was screwed.

# Chapter Fourteen

"So, when are you going to bring me back?" She leaned forward on his shoulder, and her body fought for air. The air between them was thick with the scent of sex."

"Today. Perhaps tomorrow." He lifted her chin. "Certainly, eventually."

She felt the rub of his cheek against hers and responded. "I need to restart my life again. Depending on how much press was out about my abduction, I might have to switch cities."

His kneading hands tensed on her. "What do you mean?"

"Businesses that handle financial information don't like it when their employees make the papers. They certainly don't like it when their employees return and are followed by the press."

He frowned. "What will you do?"

"Well, thanks to my involvement with the Blind Date Corporation, I have the ability to start over. It will tap me out, but I will be able to start over again in another place where folks don't know who I am. I have done it a few times."

He stroked her neck. "You aren't thinking of getting away from me, are you?"

She looked at him and shook her head. "I am going to be out of the city. Out of your life. You can find another woman with attributes similar to mine and go balls deep into her."

He growled. "These are not statements you should be making if you want me to return you to the city."

Khytten chuckled. "I believe in honesty. You will forget

about me when you meet someone else."

"And you?"

"Will learn how to serve coffee or tea or something." She shrugged. "I just need to get by."

"What about the children you care for?"

"It is constantly a changing thing. Sometimes I get repeats; other times, it is a new infant who grips my fingertip in their own. There are always children rejected by their own. I will just go looking wherever I end up."

He nodded. "Isn't it a breach of contract to move without notice while you are an active escort?"

She blinked. "How do you know . . . Zera will probably let me free."

"Yes, but your patrons need to agree if there has been no breach of their conduct."

"I don't have any regular patrons. I had two curiosities and . . . well . . . you. One date on the books is hardly a patron who will miss me."

He wrapped a hand in her hair and pulled her head back. "Repeat after me. Salat. Will. Miss. Me."

She felt her eyes widen in surprise. "Salat will miss me."

"Say it again and use your name where it should be."

She blushed. "Salat will miss Khytten."

"When I heard your name, I couldn't believe my luck. A kitten of my own." He nuzzled her cheek.

"I am sure that that isn't how the contracts work."

He grinned. "They are open to interpretation."

"I am sure that they aren't." She reached out and stroked his cheek. "Salat?"

He smiled. "It sounds good when you say it; it will sound better if you scream it, kitten."

She looked away. "I am not planning on screaming anything."

"That will make it all the sweeter."

He picked her up with his hands on her butt and his cock still lodged inside her. Every step was pleasurable torture, and when he turned and dropped onto the bed, she was astride him. Her eyes were wide, and she braced herself on his heavily muscled chest. His hands started to move her, and her senses started to spin.

He helped her to the edge, and then, he stopped.

She blinked and looked at him in shock.

He was breathing heavily, and he asked, "What do you want?"

"More." She ran her hands over all of his available skin. "I want more, Salat."

He shuddered as she whispered his name. "Then, get it yourself, kitten."

She grabbed his hands and put them on her breasts while she slowly tried to mimic the rhythm he had had going. He pulled her down to him and kissed her as she moved faster and harder. Just as she was about to cum, he rolled, pinning her to the bed and kissing her slowly. Her arms were held up and away from her over her head while he began a slow and steady thrust and retreat that was driving her insane with his care and deliberation.

He released her arms, and she held him as he provided her with slow undulating thrusts that stroked every inch of her internally. She shuddered, she gasped, she moaned, and then, she heard the whisper, "Say my name, kitten."

She blinked and groaned. "Salat."

He nipped her neck while he worked into her. "Again."

"Salat."

He coaxed her to the edge of release, and then, he bit her shoulder hard.

"Ah! Salat!" She screamed as the bite caused a wave of pain that was just what she needed to send her over the edge. She bucked, she thrashed, she moaned, and she held onto him while her body went insane.

She heard his triumphant shout, but she didn't care. Her body was wrapped in a golden cloud, and her mind was floating with it. She slowly lowered the legs that had locked around him and ran her inner thighs along his outer thighs.

He sighed happily. "That was as amazing as I had imagined. I like hearing my name from you, kitten."

She swallowed. "I certainly got that impression."

He gave her a look.

She stroked his head and brought his mouth to hers. "I got that impression, Salat."

The kiss was sweet, and it made her heart ache. If she had remained un-activated, she could have had a normal man and a normal family and a normal life. A single fat tear slid down her temple.

The kiss continued for minutes, and then, he rolled to one side, taking her with him. He slid out of her and pulled her to him. "I don't want to bring you back."

She shivered. "Reality has to start sometime. You have to go on your assignments, and I have to figure out what comes next."

He sighed. "Fine, but stay in town. I will send you funds to keep you going."

She swallowed. "That isn't why I did this, Salat."

He smiled. "I know, but if I want you where I can find you, I am more than willing to pay for the pleasure. I can send you the bounty on the active you killed. That should help you buy a house."

She blinked. "What?"

"He was worth two hundred thousand." He stroked his hand down to her breasts and moved shortly after to follow his slight touch with his mouth.

She heard a humming sound outside. "What is that noise?"

"Delivery drones. They are dropping clothing and your vehicle." He kept his attention focused on where he was. He preferred the right. She shifted to her back, and he smiled and moved across her. His thigh pressed between hers, and as he took in the calming chemicals she had dumped into the milk, he moved his thigh to press against her clit. She moaned and held tight to his head, her fingers urging him closer.

They flexed and strained together until she let out an imperceptible shiver. She felt his grin, and he continued to move between them.

She came twice more due to the steady pressure, and when she moaned, "Salat," the final time, he raised his head, and when he kissed, she got a rush of her own product. It was calming and would help her reflexes.

Bots started to whir along and brought a stack of clothing and a backpack.

He sighed. "So, a quick shower, and then, we part paths for a while."

She nodded. "Good, I am beyond sticky."

Khytten tried to sit up, but she was pinned by his head and torso. "Are you going to let me up?"

He groaned. "Fine. I am being picked up in two hours, so I will escort you as far as I can."

She blinked. "You are going?"

"I am. Aksalla calls, and I answer. I will be back here as soon as I can."

She nodded. This was what she wanted. Her freedom and his departure. Right?

The shower was slow and sweet. He washed every inch of her thoroughly; his fingers didn't miss a thing.

When he finished drying her hair, she turned and tried to wrap her hands around his cock. "Well, I can see the difficulty."

He chuckled. "I am surprised you are looking. I thought you were going to continue averting your eyes."

"It is more normal-sized than it feels."

He laughed. "It feels bigger when I am inside you?"

"For a moment when you enter, it feels like you will split me apart. Can I get dressed now?"

His eyes had narrowed, and he leaned in. "You are teasing me."

She smiled. "Yes. I get the feeling you don't get that much."

"No, I do not. I am deciding whether or not I like it or want to act on it."

"If you are going, I need to get on the road, wherever the road is."

He sighed. "Fine. I will remember the teasing the next time I book a date."

Her eyes widened. "You are still going to book me?"

"As long as you are on her roster, you can be requested by other patrons unless you are marked as exclusive. So, I have signed an exclusive contract for you while you are listed, and when you get your com back, I suggest that you agree to it." He stroked her cheek. "The terms are generous, and Blind Date's legal team has already authorized it."

She blinked. "Exclusive . . . I . . . ."

He smiled. "Get dressed. At least your motives for doing this are simply survival. I don't have to worry about you being some sultry spy out to snare me."

"They have tried that?"

"A few times. They are always . . . a bit surprised when I try and take them up on it."

She snorted, stroked her fingers down his erection, and turned to look at her clothing.

He grabbed her and pulled her against his body. "Teasing kitten."

"Just a little bit. It will probably increase as our association goes on."

He laughed. "Get dressed. Everything should fit. They were taken from your scans."

"Was there a healer here?"

"Yes. She's very good. I have used her when I needed to be patched up now and again."

She put on the miniscule thong while he sat on the edge of the bed and watched her get dressed. The nursing bra was lovely and made her mourn the torn and stained gown that she had lost. The leather pants were snug but nipped in at the waist. It was a custom fit.

"Where the hell do you get custom-fit clothing on such short notice?"

She pulled on a silky black tee and slid the outer casing of black leather over her. She could feel the armour segments in the jacket. The socks were fluffy and white with cartoon kittens, and the boots were knee-high and tight-laced.

"I look like a fetish doll for guys who like cycles." She sighed and braided her hair quickly.

He grabbed her and pressed his face between her breasts. The scooped neckline of the tee was no barrier to him. He pulled her against him, and she knelt on the bed on either side of his hips. She held his head, and they just held onto the moment. This wasn't sex. This was connection.

He got into his car, and she started the cycle. The moment they had exited the house, she knew where they were. She was forty-five minutes from the city.

She nodded to him and pulled on her helmet. The backpack had her expressing kit and a cooling unit. If she could do it on her own terms with her own equipment, she had a bit more control, and she teared up inside the helmet when it was clear that he knew it.

Control of her own body had always been lacking.

She roared down his drive, and he followed her. He knew enough about her to know that she could ride a cycle, but did he know how well?

She continued down the two-kilometre drive, and then, she turned toward the city. She was up to speed in seconds. Then, she went a little faster.

The cycle was one that she hadn't even dreamed about. It was sleek, expensive, and responded to every touch.

"*Kitten, what are you doing?*"

"Seeing what this cycle can do, Salat." She purred it

through the com in her helmet.

His sleek desert runner pulled up next to her, and he shook his head slightly. *"You are being reckless."*

"Check my files again. I used to test vehicles for a living. This is just a test."

She lowered herself over the controls, and her arms slid forward for high speed. She passed cars like they were standing still and moving like she was on a mission.

*"You do know what you are doing, kitten. I will leave you there. Head to Blind Date Corporation. They will help you find quarters and help you get in touch with law enforcement."*

She said, "Thank you, Salat. How do I get the cycle back to you?"

*"Oh, that? It's yours. I don't like them. Too dangerous."* He chuckled. *"See you soon, kitten."*

She chuckled and slowed to a more reasonable speed as she entered the city.

Zera's voice came to her. *"Salat gave me your com frequency. You are heading to Blind Date?"*

"Yeah. I have no clothes, my com was blown up, and I need to park a cycle."

*"Those are things that can be fixed. I will also have the examiner come here to interview you."*

"Right now?"

*"Sure. Better to get it over with."*

Khytten drove directly to the hub, and Zera talked her over to the loading dock. The cycle drove neatly into the cargo elevator, and they headed up.

Zera was wearing dark clothing, and her mood was sombre.

Khytten pulled her helmet off. "What's happened?"

"My sister passed. It seems she wasn't free of the effects of the doll maker's attack as we had hoped. The funeral is tomorrow."

"Oh, Zera. I am so sorry."

"Thank you. At least she passed the program. That was what she always wanted."

They arrived on the Blind Date floor, and Khytten pushed the cycle to one side.

"Salat's cycle?"

Khytten blushed. "No, he . . . uh . . . gave it to me. He doesn't like them."

"But he knew you did and got you leathers and a helmet as well. I like him more and more. We will get you into something business-suit-like."

"Okay, let's go play dress-up. Can you help me find out if my com was retrieved?"

"The examiner should know. They probably went through it looking for incriminating messages."

"Oh. What about the communication from here?"

"Extraordinarily encrypted. Nothing from us except your deposits."

"Oh. That could look bad."

"Well, you now have proof your patron likes to give you exorbitant gifts. You are getting along well with Salat?"

"Um, yes? He mentioned an exclusivity contract."

"Yes, it is on record here, but you obviously haven't had the means to sign it. I mean, if you wanted to sign it."

She bit her lip. "I like Salat, don't get me wrong, but he is a bit much."

Zera looked at her as they moved toward Khytten's wardrobe.

"No, not that. He definitely wants me for my body. But there is something else in his eyes. Like he never thought to find anyone either. That is kinda scary. I get the feeling that he isn't going to let me out of his sight or, at least, out of his monitoring range." She wasn't sure, but she thought that her jacket chuckled.

She sat at a small table in a business suit tailored to fit her, and she smiled as the examiner sat across from her.

"Good afternoon."

He smiled and nodded. "Good afternoon. Miss Danforth?"

"Correct."

"I am Examiner Tell. Pleased to meet you."

She extended her hand to his, and his eyes went wide at the contact.

When his gaze fixed on her chest, she knew what kind of examiner he was. Contact exam.

"How much can you see?"

"Six hours."

She nodded. "I was rescued by my patron."

He released her hand and rubbed his fingers together. "You and he are close?"

"At intervals. My abduction was crafted by the Mentor, though. My patron doesn't have to kidnap me; he just has to book me."

"Maybe he was tired of paying."

She stared at the examiner. "He is out of town now and is offering me funds so that I can get a new place."

"You are content to be under his thumb?"

"He has a very talented thumb. But, none of the people or places around here offer help to the working poor. You are either successful or ground under a boot."

He checked his notes. "You are a wetnurse?"

She snorted. "I am a data entry clerk. I donate milk to the neonatal unit of the hospital and a few other children's charities."

He frowned. "Your other employer did not notice you were missing."

"I know I have probably been fired. Two days gone without calling in isn't acceptable to them."

"We can notify them that you were abducted."

"It won't do much good. I will wrap up my employment with them over a call." She grimaced. "If I do stay there, I will have to answer questions, and I don't want to relive the experience over and over again."

"Well, I will record this, so hopefully, we only need to do it once."

She nodded and explained waking shackled up and the guy molesting her. She also did not conceal her counterattack.

"My patron said I would get the bounty on the dead guy, so that is more start-over funding."

He smiled and said, "It is doubtful that an attack like that would be worth . . . holy shit."

Tell looked at her in surprise. "The bounty has been issued by the government offices and deposited in your accounts. The bounty was not only for the man that you described. One point five million has been deposited for your part in finding and expunging a criminal stronghold."

She nearly fell off her chair. "What?"

"Hunting active criminals is a definitely lucrative occupation. Now, I need the name of your patron for confirmation."

Zera walked in and handed him a slip of paper and then walked out.

The examiner looked at the paper and then looked at Khytten. "Salat? The Demon Cat of Aksalla? He is your patron?"

She nodded.

He exhaled and made notes. "At least the massacre in the desert now makes sense. So, he found you and rescued you?"

"More or less. The criminals had made free with me while I was unconscious, and some items had to be removed. Then we negotiated the price of my freedom, and he still hasn't told me what that is."

"Perhaps he was joking, Miss."

"That is doubtful. He does not joke when it comes to doing jobs. I was a job."

"I don't think that was the case, Miss."

She snorted. "He also doesn't like other people playing with his toys. That was probably it. Frankly. I blame his mother."

Zera's snort came from inside her office.

The examiner just looked at her, asked a few more questions, and made a hasty retreat.


Salat finished listening to the interview in his audio implant, and he grinned as he lunged out to take care of another terrorist cell with hostages. His little kitten meeting his mother would be something to see. Bitter steel versus angry fluff. It was something he was going to make happen.

# Chapter Fifteen

Zera breathed a sigh of relief that Khytten was back and safe. When the examiner left, Khytten looked around and winced. "Do you need any help in here?"

"Uh, if you have time." Khytten said, "I am going to have to go down to the peacekeeper depot to get my com."

"Why?"

"It is broken. They need to issue me a writ to get a new one."

Zera looked at her warily. "That's weird."

"Is it? I know you are probably swamped, but can you come with me? In like, ten minutes."

Khytten looked nervous, her fingers were tangled together, and she looked oddly embarrassed.

"Sure. Why ten... oh." Khytten needed to make a withdrawal. "Take twenty. Keep the business suit, though. Folks are less likely to mess with you. High heels though. That keeps them from dismissing you. You want them to look."

"Yes, Ma'am." She left.

Fifteen minutes she was back wearing four-inch heels with her hair up in a twist and a curl cascading down her shoulder against her neck with very obvious bright dots visible.

Zera laughed. "He bit you?"

"Yeah. He doesn't drink blood, so this was just for fun." She grumbled. "I thought it might cement the idea that I have been engaged in frisky behaviour after my apartment blew up."

"The examiner won't be there."

"I know, but it is in my file already. Peacekeepers gossip like teenagers. I saw the news. My connection to the Blind Date Corporation was already divulged based on information in my shattered com. They went through it and found everything they could. If I have to be an expensive escort, I am going to look like one." She sighed. "I am going to have to go shopping. I hate shopping."

Zera laughed at the disgust in her face. She opened a file. "Dainty drew these up for you, but we never had a client that would need them. What do you think?"

Khytten inhaled sharply. "Those are so pretty . . . and so slutty." The woman drew her head back sharply. "He's listening and talking. What do you mean you had it put in during the healing? I can so be trusted on my own."

Zera snorted as she caught on to what the one-sided conversation indicated. "You have an implant."

Khytten looked at her. "Apparently, and it contains a chatty fucker. Wait. Are you killing people while you are talking to me? No, I am not going to describe the clothes. No, I am not. Shut up now. The guy you just hit is gargling a lot. You might want to get on that. Okay. That's better. Keep the eavesdropping to a minimum. No, I am not going to do that. No, it doesn't count as a date. Go back to work."

Zera laughed. "He had a live com implanted in you?"

She grimaced. "Apparently. Thank god he doesn't have visuals."

"Let's go to the depot and get you back in touch with the normal world instead of your patron."

Khytten held up a finger. "Yes, I know that the contract is waiting, and I am sure you were very generous. Yes, I will thank you properly when I see you."

Zera snorted and got her jacket. "The transport is waiting."

They left together and sat in the transport. When they arrived at the depot, Zera went first. Khytten walked with her, and Zera was happy when the woman introduced herself at the desk.

"Ah, Miss Danforth. Please, come this way."

Zera moved to accompany Khytten, and when the desk officer stopped her, Zera said, "Pursuant to Code sixteen dash three, any citizen is entitled to a companion when dealing with the peacekeepers in a non-criminal capacity. You are not taking her anywhere alone."

The officer blinked. "Yes, Ma'am."

Zera walked with Khytten, and they went to the rear of the office where a captain's private office waited for them. This was definitely unusual. They had just been walked past the entire shop. Khytten smiled politely. "Captain Minwell? I was told I needed to come here to get my shattered com and a writ that says it was broken while I was the victim of a criminal action."

The captain leaned back and looked her over, and then, he looked to Zera. "Who are you?"

"Researcher Zera."

He looked over her dismissively, and then, it struck him. "You are the one from the interview. The nympho who was on Torun."

"Not a nympho; I just don't have to play the monogamy game. It is rather refreshing. If you weren't in a relationship, I would suggest that you try it yourself." Zera smiled. "I am also the owner of Z-Tech, and I have made all the weapons in this building. I would watch your next words very carefully."

The captain scowled. "This is a bit of paperwork. Please, have a seat."

Zera noted that the chairs had been moved back eighteen inches. She glanced up and saw the security camera positioned to look down Khytten's shirt. She grabbed the chairs and moved them close to the desk.

Khytten looked at her with a frown.

"Ah, the security camera from the hallway was at a particularly bad angle . . . for you," Zera murmured.

"Ah. Right. That again." She sat, and Zera sat next to her.

Zera looked around, and there was a casually moving line of guys who were trying to get a look at Khytten. So, the word was out as to what her active status was.

"Miss Danforth, was there any reason that you didn't register as an active?"

Khytten sighed. "Yes. Being marked as an active makes folks look at you to determine what form it took. I was already tired of being looked at, and my situation didn't warrant being added to the program. Folks—men especially—look at me and draw certain inferences because some glands grew abnormally large. I can't control it, I am not fond of it, and being treated like a freak is not on my list of things to do today."

She smiled pleasantly at the captain, whose gaze was buried in her cleavage. "It seems some idiots can't look past the tits."

He jerked his gaze up, and he grinned and then frowned. "Did you just insult me?"

"I don't know. The insult would only land if you were staring at my chest. So, as you are a respectable peacekeeper, who is out for the benefit of those under their care, including me, can you please start the process so I can replace my com?"

He blinked and nodded. "Right. So, you were in your apartment, according to the report."

"I was."

"There was a gift box on the floor."

"There was."

"It was from an expensive boutique."

She mourned the loss of the gown and robe. "I have no doubt."

"Who was it from?"

"My patron."

"Does he often send you gifts?"

"That was the first time. My first gift from him, and it was torn up and then torn up some more. I was upset."

"So, this is a man who pays to have sex with you?"

Khytten smiled. "Eventually."

"How much does that cost?"

Khytten paused. She knew how much showed up in her account but wasn't sure how much Blind Date took off the top. "Zera?"

"Miss Danforth's presence commands a price of fifteen thousand for a four-hour span. The corporation takes twenty percent for administration and wardrobe."

The captain's eyes bugged out. "For four hours?"

Zera chuckled. "Of course. All of my escorts, male or female, have to have active capabilities that make them suitable sexual partners for folks who are strong, fast, or have particular requirements. Some are declared and some are not. Khytten's patron had been on the books for a while, and after she had a few trial dates with other patrons, they had a date, and it went well."

*"Very well."* His voice rumbled through her skull. She tried not to jump.

"So, he sent you a three-thousand-dollar negligee?"

She mourned the loss all over again. "Aw, man. It's worse than I thought. It was so pretty."

*"I will get you another. A wardrobe full, though that would be more for me than for you."*

She smiled slightly. The captain was riveted, and it seemed to be her expression that did it.

She spoke. "Captain? Is there anything else?"

He shook his head to clear it. "Yes. Um, you were abducted after your apartment exploded. Where were you taken?"

"One of the deserts. It was hot when I woke up."

"How did you get free?"

"Ah. My patron came to get me."

Zera nodded. "I contacted him when the news caused an alert on my com. There was no way for me to get to her, but he has more resources available to him. He brought her back, relatively intact."

The snort in her ear made her smile. *"Given more time, I could have done so much more."*

She shivered and was glad that her jacket was covering her nipples. She didn't want to draw any more attention than she was already.

"Relatively?"

Khytten smiled. "He got a little bitey, but I heal quickly."

*"Sorry, not sorry. Shall I put an end to this?"*

She exhaled in her sexiest tone. "Please, Patron."

The captain's com went off, and Khytten looked to Zera.

Warily, the captain answered the call on a handset, and as the call went on, the captain's expression grew slightly fearful.

Zera smiled. "I know that face. Salat's on the line."

The com went loud, and the captain was horrified. *"Hello, kitten. Feeling well? I will be done with my out-of-town work tomorrow and look forward to seeing you."*

She fought the heat in her cheeks. "I would check to see the booking, but I don't have my com yet."

*"Ah, the good captain will set you up with that. If he doesn't, he and I will have a conversation when I return to the capitol, and I don't think that he wants that to happen, isn't that correct, Captain?"*

The captain swallowed and nodded. "Correct, Agent Salat. She will have her com in a moment."

*"Oh, while I wait. Please proceed. I will end the call when she has her com and not before. Also, tell your men to stop staring at them. It is rude."* Salat's low voice rolled out of the com.

Zera was chuckling.

Khytten grinned. "Suddenly, I want an *I heart the Demon Cat of Aksalla* t-shirt."

He purred smoothly, *"Whatever you want, kitten. Your wishes are my desires, and I have very poor impulse control around you."*

The captain realized that this was rapidly turning into a session between lovers, and he opened his drawer. "Here is the com. Here is the writ from us and the one from the teams."

Her mouth fell open slightly, and she snapped it shut. "Right. Well. Thanks."

*"You need to sign for it, kitten."* His tone was gentle.

"Oh. Right." She looked to the man behind the desk.

The captain fluttered around and showed a signature tablet to her. She got up and signed for it.

*"Captain, please, don't look down her blouse. The positioning of the cameras in the depot is particularly unfortunate. It is almost like you set a trap for a victim of abduction and assault, but you wouldn't do that, now would you?"*

The captain looked positively green. "You can see me?"

*"I have intercepted your feed and directed all of the cameras to you. They are going to remain that way until you begin to understand a bit of what my kitten goes through. It is not fun to be watched at all times. The feeds will randomly display your office to folk in the depot. You can be in it or not, but the spotlight will still be there. It will end when I feel like it or when kitten asks me to stop, and she will have to ask me very nicely."*

"Stop being such an asshole." She grumped. "Just turn the surveillance on randomly when he is at his desk. Or entering or leaving the men's room."

Laughter filled the room. *"There are your claws."*

She nodded to Zera. "I have the com and the writs. We can go now."

Zera's shoulders were shaking as Salat singsonged out, *"Have fun, kitten."*

"Jackass!" She called it out as they left the room.

"*Miss you, too!*"

"It has been six hours!"

"*I am counting the minutes as well, kitten. Have fun with Zera.*"

"I am leaving now!"

He was laughing uproariously as the office door closed behind them.

Zera was laughing so hard that Khytten had to support her as they headed out to their transport. The com registry office was across the street, and they went to get the replacement. It was fairly smooth with the writs to get the new com unit, and Khytten splurged for the best model available, recommended by Zera.

Once she had her small communicator and projector, she felt better. It was like she had been naked, but now the flat cuff was in place with all her data, accounts, and correspondence available.

"*Now, kitten, sign that contract.*"

She grumbled. "Fine. When is your birthday?"

She and Zera were in the transport.

"*Why, what does it matter?*"

Khytten chuckled, and Zera looked at her when she said, "Free, no-holds-barred sex on your birthday until you are sated or I pass out, whichever comes first or last, I guess. Non-transferrable if you are out of town."

"*You are trying to kill me, aren't you?*"

"Absolutely not, but rules are rules."

He began to whisper in her head all the delightfully depraved things he would do to her. It was like when he had been invisible and his lips were next to her ear. Her pulse quickened the same way.


Zera looked at what was rapidly becoming a friend and laughed at her appalled expression. It reminded her of her first dates with Torun. He had trouble letting go, but once he did, it was like she had unleashed a beast that loved rough sex and cuddling. When she thought back to the early days, she remembered her being in a daze most of the time and Torun showing up at her door after every clash and intervention, wanting attention. He noticed the power that she gave him when they had sex, and he wanted to be the best that he could be and enjoy an actual relationship at the same time.

Dating someone on the teams was forbidden, and she was charged, and he was put on a warning. That was when Blind Date was created. For it to be a legal escort arrangement, she needed to open membership and have more escorts. She and Susara discovered that there was a true need for the service, and the company grew. The training regimen for new recruits took trial and error, but if they could make it through the vids and practical, chances were that they could make it through a date while blindfolded.

"Khytten, would you like to go out for dinner?"

"I couldn't take up more of your time. You have a funeral tomorrow."

"Sweetie, you can help me forget; plus, Torun keeps trying to get me to move in with him, and I have no idea where he actually lives. I think I am better off in town for now."

She gave directions to the transport and made a call. Her usual table for two would be ready in half an hour.

"Khytten, did you want to dress for dinner?"

Khytten perked up. "That sounds fun."

"Dress-up is one of the best parts of the job."

Khytten's colour began to rapidly rise. "He would disagree. Hell, he is disagreeing."

"He can do what he likes, but I can put together a signal jammer if he keeps interrupting. He can listen, but he needs to stop commenting."

Khytten tilted her head and nodded. "He agrees. He was

just playing with a new toy."

Zera smiled. "What did you promise him?"

"Absolutely nothing."

"Fine, what did he ask for?"

"Oh, he just wants to listen in at private moments."

The transport pulled up at the corporate headquarters, and they left it and headed inside. Time to do a five-minute makeover and hit the town for a nice meal.

Zera looked at her friend and grinned. "Well-chosen, Kit."

"Kit?"

"It is shorter and cute. You deserve a cute name. Did you sign the contract?"

"I did." She pressed a hand to her ear and blushed. Salat must be expressing his enthusiasm.

"Excellent. Torun was starting to get interested, and since Salat wants you to be exclusive, that would get messy. They would probably both survive but not if Torun gets his head cut off."

Zera finished applying her lipstick and smiled. "Ready when you are."

They linked arms and headed back down to their new luxury transport, which glided smoothly away once they were inside.

"So, do you go out for dinner like this often?" Kit smiled.

"Not as often as I used to. Life has gotten away from me. I need to get it back so that I enjoy it a bit more." Zera chuckled. "Also, I like to show off. We are stunning and ostensibly available. What they don't know might drive up clientele."

Kit laughed. "Well, then, what do you suggest?"

"Don't be shocked if I suggest that we kiss."

Kit muttered, "No, I will not take pictures of that. Not even if you beg. No bargaining. Yes, I am guessing that if she is asking, it is because it will be on the news or in a tabloid or something."

Zera laughed. "I will see what I can arrange. So, Kit, when is your birthday?"

"Uh, a week from this Thursday."

"Nice. What do you want?"

"What?"

"For your birthday. What do you want as a present?" Zera smiled slyly.

"You are evil."

Zera laughed. "Which one of us are you talking to?"

"Both."

"Well, what is it. What do you want for your birthday?"

"I . . . don't celebrate it. My activation kicked in on my birthday, and that was when my life went to shit. Next thing I knew, I was checked into activation camp and then came the lawsuit, and I was on my own. I see it as the start of a disaster, not something to be celebrated. Maybe I should put up a cenotaph and deal with it that way."

"Oh, Khytten. I am sorry." Zera took her hand.

"No, it's not a problem. I know you will probably be back to business as usual, but I wouldn't mind another girls' night out. I don't have much of that in my life."

Zera smiled. "I think I can arrange something."

"Why am I suddenly uneasy? The look on your face is chilling."

"Because you are very smart, Kit." Zera patted her leg. "Now, let's have dinner, and we can talk about your party."

"Party?" There was panic in her eyes.

"Yeah. I think this is going to be quite the event."

"Zera, no, please, I will do anything, but no party."

"Oh, you beg so sweetly; no wonder Salat is smitten."

Zera could tell that Salat was laughing as Khytten covered her face. She would have a nice party with patrons and other escorts, no masks required, but the escorts could wear them if they wanted. She really hoped that Salat could make it, or their contract was going to be the subject of conversation frequently as the patrons got one look in Khytten's eyes and were smitten by her shy innocence.

# Chapter Sixteen

Halfway through dinner, Zera needed to ask, "Kit, will you come to Susa's funeral tomorrow?"

Kit looked at her with wide eyes. "I don't want to intrude."

"I need all the friends there that I can get." Zera added in a low singsong. "I can get you some light weaponry."

Kit's eyes glowed. "You can?"

"Sure. I have a bunch in my research and development department. Better than peacekeeper issue. Pulse weapons with fast recovery time."

Kit looked at her, all breathy. "Zera, are you trying to seduce me?"

Zera laughed. "No, but it's nice to know your sweet spot. What would you do for a rocket launcher?"

Kit leaned in and whispered with her hand over one ear so it would muffle what Salat could hear.

Zera listened to the graphic proposition, and Zera blinked in surprise. "Wow. That's . . . detailed. Sorry, Salat, I am going to have to cancel your exclusive contract. Her mouth alone could make millions."

Zera laughed when her com lit up with angry threats.

Kit whispered, "She was kidding, Patron. I don't cheat once I have made up my mind."

Zera handed a recording unit to the server. "Take a video, please."

Kit leaned toward her, and Zera turned her head and kissed her with a slow kiss that rapidly got out of control. Kit whimpered, and Zera blinked and lifted her head. "Oh, wow. It's a shame I never got to sleep with you."

The server was standing there with a hot blush on her cheeks, and she handed the recording unit back. "Thank you, ladies."

Zera grinned. "I think we have improved her world outlook."

"What are you doing?"

Zera uploaded the video to Salat's account. "I promised him a copy of the kiss. Damn, I wish that I could have gotten to you before the contract."

Kit asked, "Uh, why?"

"Because my activity is to enhance others. I increase power and precision."

"How?"

"With pleasure. Giving or receiving." Zera grinned. "I can go either way."

Kit sat still.

"What is he saying?" Zera was smirking.

"It isn't really words; it is just a long, low growl."

She giggled, and they saw the dessert cart. A look from Zera, and it was brought over. They showed it no mercy.

In the transport back to the base, Kit asked, "Do you always eat on the VIP platform?"

"That is up to the discretion of the restauranteur. They can put us up there or in the back. Today, we looked good, and the kiss got quite a bit of attention. How is Salat's situation?"

Kit smiled slightly. "I think he's purring."

Zera laughed. He had always been horribly intimidating, and she was never invited on a date by him. It turned out she literally wasn't his type. Kit was his ideal woman, and there was a lot more to her than there appeared to be at first glance. Her fascination with weaponry was eye-opening.

They headed back to BDC, and in the elevator, Zera asked, "Did you want to see those weapons?"

"Sure, but I have to take care of things for a few minutes."

"Oh. Right. So, you are pretty much tethered then." Having a physical restraint would be rough.

"Well, Salat got me a backpack with a pump kit in a really quiet design. It does a good job, too."

"What does it feel like?"

Kit laughed. "Like two suction cups attached to your tits pulling rhythmically. No romance, a little bit of hormonal action, and embarrassing. I can show you a fun trick if you can find two shot glasses."

Zera blinked. "A trick? Like what?"

"I can capture an orgasm in a glass, but the process is going to be embarrassing."

Intrigued, she said, "What will it take?"

"I can express a bit when I orgasm, and it freezes the hormones in that moment."

"Ask Salat if I can help." Zera smiled.

Kit blushed. "He said yes if he can listen."

"If we put masks on, we can record it, and he can watch."

Kit winced. "Uh, he said yes."

Zera got to watch Kit's milk-white skin writhing and undulating as she took in pleasure and power. When she came, the glasses filled, and Zera helped her right them.

The hit of the milk on Zera's tongue dropped her to her knees. Liquid pleasure ran through her blood, and she shuddered hard as her thighs clenched and her channel flexed. "Ohmygod. Where have you been all my life?"

Kit laughed and handed her the second shot. "I have already had mine. Go ahead."

"How about we share it?" Zera took the shot and kissed Kit, causing her to flinch and moan when the milk hit her tongue.

They both shuddered and moaned. Zera shared what she could while she held herself upright.

She sat back and looked at Kit. "When did you learn you

could do that?"

"I learned about the mood transfer when I was a teenager. It's why I am usually so calm. I try and keep my emotions on the bright side. When I go dark, so does the emotion in the milk." Kit chuckled. "I am usually too tired to masturbate, so I had nearly forgotten about the orgasm thing until Salat reminded me."

"Yeah, that seems like the kind of thing he would notice."

"Right, now I need to actually pump. This is getting messy. Kit reached for her bag and tidied up before attaching the pumps to her breasts. She flicked them on, and the collection unit began to extract.

"Why does the suction pulse?"

"Two reasons. It mimics human consumption, and it reduces the chance of burst blood vessels and mastitis."

Zera watched and then thanked Kit for the demonstration. She went back to her office and made some arrangements for Kit's birthday party. That girl really deserved to be celebrated.

The next morning was obnoxiously cheerful. Zera was dressed in a mourning dress, and Kit was at her side wearing black. They stood near the casket for a moment before it was closed, and then, they followed it to the front bench. Torun arrived, and Kit moved aside to let him sit next to Zera.

There were people from the program, team members, business moguls, and admirers, as well as friends of Susara's parents. Words were spoken, music played, and Susa remained still and silent at the front of the chapel.

Zera felt big, fat tears streaking down her cheeks, and she held Torun's hand during the service. She was numb. The line afterward was intense. Folks hugged her, shook her hand, stroked her cheek, and Kit stood just behind her through the whole thing.

When she needed to touch up her makeup, Kit went with

her, and they were standing by the sinks when the door started to glow.

Kit took a step toward it with a weapon drawn. When someone came out of the portal, she shot, once to the leg, once to the head.

Zera was stunned at how calmly Kit pulled the trigger.

"Do we want out of here?" Kit's voice was bland.

"We do."

Kit shot into the portal, and another figure fell. "Right. Stand away from the wall."

She took the weapon, twisted the control, and aimed it at the wall for a concussive blast. Four quick repeats, and they were out of the ladies' room and standing near the parking lot. Kit quietly adjusted the weapon again, and they walked back to the crowd at the front of the chapel.

The funeral director came up to Zera and said, "We are proceeding to the mausoleum, Miss. If you are ready?"

Zera looked back at the direction they had come from and didn't see any incoming personnel. "Yes, that is . . . I am ready."

The casket was carried out on the shoulders of six of Susara's patrons. They walked out of the chapel and down the gravel laneway. Zera's gaze and senses were on high alert. Torun was one of the pallbearers, and she kept her gaze fixed on him.

Kit walked beside and behind her, but she was alert as well. It was nice to have someone have her back for no other reason than that they were friends.

"Something is going to happen."

Kit snorted. "I know. Salat is cursing a blue streak. He's surprisingly inventive for someone who doesn't like cussing."

"Well, we are going to a place with only one door."

Kit chuckled. "I think I can pay for any damages."

"Don't worry about the damages; I can wear it."

"Oh good. I am out of practice."

"It didn't look that way."

"I guess it is like riding a cycle." Kit smiled.

Zera sighed and watched them carry Susara into the family mausoleum and set next to her parents. When she had put three roses on her family caskets, she stepped out, and the stone door was set in place.

Susa was gone. Kit caught her as she slumped and brought her over to Torun. Zera smiled. Kit smelled like peaches and cream. It was comforting and hard to leave her when Zera was handed over.

Kit smiled and walked a few feet away, only to be surrounded by men from some of the teams.

Zera didn't hear what she said, but she knew that Salat did, and anyone who stepped out of line would be spoken to politely but firmly at a later time.

"How are you holding up, Zera?" Torun's voice was quiet.

"Pretty well, I think. Kit has been a godsend. She is charming, witty, and distracting as can be."

He let out a low sigh. "There is a certain fresh-faced charm to her."

"Yeah, but I wouldn't entertain any ideas. Her patron just signed an exclusive contract with her."

"I am sure I could ask him to spare a night."

Zera giggled. "I am sure you couldn't. Her patron doesn't get along with you."

He looked at her with wide eyes. "*He* has an escort? I thought he was too freaky for that."

"He was put on a supply file. He made specific requests, and when those requests were fulfillable, he was contacted, and he made a date." Zera grinned. "I am happy for them both. She's a hard fit as well."

He wrapped an arm around her waist. "So, have you given any thought to my invitation?"

"I have, and I prefer to be in a place I can get away from."

"You will have to give in to me eventually."

She wrapped her arms around him and hugged him. "I know. But I have to finish the company expansion first, and that means more personnel, which means interviews."

"I am beginning to regret my suggestion."

"Without it, we would be facing charges again. It is easier to be your whore than your girlfriend."

His arms tightened around her. "I don't like that term."

"I know, but it is the one the government lets me live with. Team members can't have relationships, but they can pay for relief, remember? It was a fun loophole that we found."

"It is frustrating."

"Yeah, but you have been able to try so many more lovers this way."

"And I always come back to you. You are my choice, every time." He pressed a kiss to the top of her head. "Though your friend Kit offers some interesting options."

She chuckled. "You have no idea, and you won't. Salat will skin you alive if you try."

"Shit. Salat? I thought she was Morniger's."

"You fear an auditor more than being sliced to pieces?"

He laughed. "Every day of the week."

Kit walked back to her and said, "I have to, uh . . ."

"Yeah. Got it. I will wait here with Torun. Torun, this is Kit."

He extended his hand and took hers in his. Zera watched her face as Kit tracked the hand being raised to Torun's lips. He left a light kiss on her knuckles, and she stood politely until he let her go.

"Pleased to meet you, Team Leader Torun. Please excuse me." She bobbed a short bow and smiled. Kit scampered off, avoiding hands that tried to reach out for her, and Zera didn't think she even noticed that she avoided contact.

"Wow. She's so wholesome."

"And she also shot two men in the ladies' room with less

emotion than her applying her mascara."

He tensed, and she winced. "What?"

"A portal opened in the ladies' room. Kit shot the men coming through. We are about to be under attack, or someone is trying to kidnap me."

He nodded. "Or Kit."

Zera's eyes widened, and she ran into the chapel and the room where Kit had set up her pack. There was spilled milk and blood in the chamber. Oh, Salat was going to be pissed.

She turned and looked at Torun. "They got her."

"She's the lactator?"

"Yeah. If they can convince her to cooperate, they will be able to access the limbic centres of anyone they can get the milk into. They can brainwash an entire city block using one coffee shop."

His shock was obvious in his features. "That's dangerous. I haven't heard of a registered active with that capability."

"She wasn't registered. Her parents found her active transformation embarrassing and left her when she was just a child. She has filled out the minimal amount of paperwork to get by."

"And has never been on record, so no one knows her capabilities."

"I have run some tests, and her biology is remarkably adaptable." Zera brought up her com and winced when the angry tone rolled through.

"You were supposed to keep her safe, Zera. She's in the warehouse district, and her system is in distress." Salat's voice growled at her.

"I know, Salat. It is my sister's funeral. I thought they would come for me, not her."

"I am heading there now. Feel free to send backup."

"Yes, Salat. On its way."

Torun nodded. "I've got this. Get to the transport."

She nodded, and he gave the team members at the funeral the briefing. Five minutes later, they were on their way; the fliers went ahead for recon in their formal uniforms, looking like dark angels.

Torun looked at the site, and he whistled softly. "Salat is losing his touch. No one is bleeding."

Zera was looking for the pale limbs in the forty bodies, and when she didn't find them, she smiled. "It wasn't Salat. This was Kit."

Torun blinked. "What?"

"She didn't complete her peacekeeper's exam, but she was a fully trained peacekeeper. She also likes weapons."

An angry Salat stalked in, walked right past them, and headed for a collection of barrels. He reached down and pulled out a bloody and dishevelled Kit. "My heart nearly stopped when you started shooting."

"I am a really good shot." She squeaked as he hugged her tightly. "No . . . don't!"

He glanced down between them and chuckled. "Come on, kitten, and let's get you sorted."

She crossed her arms over her chest, and the small blast weapons were still in her hands.

Zera let them pass, as did the army of team members who came to help. "Um, I guess we start identifying bodies?"

Torun chuckled. "I guess so. Women like her take all the fun out of being a hero."

"That is just because Salat gets to comfort her, and you don't."

"Probably. Why were they after your friend?" Hron stepped up.

"Kit has tremendous power. When they get back in here, she is going to have to get registered." Zera sighed. "Kit is not going to like that."

"Why not?"

"She is an unidentified classification. An at-will booster who can create modifications."

"Salat didn't look any different. Angrier, maybe." He chuckled.

"She doesn't want him to change. She likes him just the way he is but will probably keep him healthy and healing rapidly." She smiled. "I just don't want to see her ground up by the program. She hasn't had good experiences with it yet."

The teams started recording the massacre.

Someone asked, "Where did she get the weapons?"

Zera grinned. "I gave them to her. They were created by one of the Z-tech designers."

Kolij frowned, a storm cloud over his head. "No, physically, where were they? I find it hard to believe they didn't notice it when they grabbed her."

Zera looked at him, made guns with her fingers, and tucked them under her breasts. "Like that. There were also six extra charge packs on each side."

His eyes widened. "Right, so she is that . . . uh . . . well-endowed."

There was the sound of a vehicle powering up, and Zera sighed. "And there she goes. I think he is going to offer some first aid and a safe place to recover."

Torun and those in earshot snorted.

Zera looked at the carnage. "Well, she was right. She is a very good shot. She might have gotten more dates at first if that was on her escort profile."

Kolij grinned. "I would have gone for it."

Bothin nudged his arm. "Eleven is a wonderful woman. She deserves more humanity than folks accord her. She's sweet and shy and very generous."

"And she's now exclusive to Salat, so be extra sure he isn't around if you are discussing her attributes."

Bothin smiled. "She got rid of my allergies."

Zera looked at the giant hulk of a man, and she smiled. "Yeah, that seems like the kind of thing she would do."

Torun wrapped her in his arms, and he asked her, "What

are you going to do now?"

"Ah. Me? I am going to kill Mentor, the doll maker, and anyone else who had a hand in Susara's death."

She turned to him and wrapped her arms around his neck, smiling. "Care to join me, purple pretty?"

He kissed her, and their tongues tangled and slid against each other while he lifted her up. When they came up for air, he whispered, "I can't directly help you if you are breaking the law, vigilante-style."

"Can you watch my back in case I fail?"

He grinned. "That I can do. Where are you going?"

"Kit got the coordinates from them while they were torturing her. Salat just sent the conversation to my com with an order not to put his kitten in danger again."

He smiled slowly. "You know where Mentor is?"

"I do."

"Why are you still here?"

"Because I need a hug before I go do what I have to do."

He hugged her carefully. "Go do what you have to do."

She laughed. "I will. Give me a five-minute head start. I am wearing heels."

"Fine. Ping me when you get there."

"Will do."

She turned when he caught her arm. "What?"

"You are going to have to pay for this."

Zera shrugged. "I know. I am willing to pay. This guy has to go."

He kissed her once more, and then, he followed her as she walked outside. Time to blow her cover.

# Chapter Seventeen

Zera bent forward on the street, focused on her destination, and shot forward. Superspeed was hard to manage, but it got her where she needed to go in under two minutes. Running through the unpopulated areas made her less likely to hit someone, but she ended up where she had found Susa's body, her chest heaving, and her funeral clothes smouldering gently.

She walked to the nearest building and opened the door to the coffee shop, walking through and into the janitor's closet. The staircase that shouldn't be there was exactly where the man who had been cutting Kit said it was.

Kit worked fast, and she had no problem doing what had to be done at the drop of a hat. From the time she had been captured, she had offered her torturer invulnerability but given him truth serum. The address had been easy to obtain, and that is when Kit started shooting. The precise location was the one thing Zera hadn't found, and Kit got it for her. She was getting a fruit basket if Salat let her surface again.

Zera headed down the steps, and she sent out a stun wave that knocked most of the men and women out cold. She continued producing those waves in a pulse as she walked into the throne room where Mentor was seated.

"Now, this is what I expected. Where is the doll maker?"

He smiled slightly. "To your right, in that pile you just made. I thought you would be more careful."

"You thought wrong."

She walked up to him, and his eyes intensified. "Where are you sending them?"

181

"To the tops of buildings. You can't save them all."

She raised her hand and said, "Mother would have been so disappointed in you."

He stood up. "I could say the same."

Deadly disk was not something she would ever use in a normal room, but it severed Mentor in half. Anyone in a fifty-foot radius from her would have been sliced in two.

He slid to the floor, and she cut his skull in half with a blade pulse. The active that had given her that power had died years earlier, but it was very effective.

Zera scraped the pieces of him together and burned them in a DNA-eradicating fire. No one could be allowed to investigate him.

People around the room started to sit up.

She wandered around the room, and when she found the active she was looking for, she smiled. "Hello, doll maker."

He looked at her in surprise. "How do you know who I am?"

"I have seen you. I have seen you with Mentor. I have seen you with escort Two. I have seen you drawing the souls out of your victims and laugh as their bodies dropped to be used as vessels for Mentor. Why did you attack Two?"

"I . . . I was just following orders."

She leaned in and whispered, "You laughed when she fell. You let her soul fly free, and they dumped her dying body for me to find."

He stepped back. "He wanted to get your attention. He realized he had chosen the wrong escort."

She smiled slightly. "Yeah, he was an idiot."

"Was?"

"Yeah. He's dead. You're next."

"What? You can't."

She grinned. "Who says I can't? I am not a team member, I am a researcher, and you are my experiment. Let's see how you feel with your soul ripped out of your body. I haven't done this before, so it's going to hurt."

She reached into his head and grabbed his consciousness, emotional register, and spirit of creativity, and then, she pulled it out of his skull while he screamed.

The team members burst into the lair a moment later, and she smiled and let the soul go. "Oops. I could probably have done that more neatly."

She knelt with her hands behind her head as Torun cuffed her, and he sighed. "You should have killed him before we arrived, Zera."

She chuckled. "There were a lot of things I should have done, but now, I don't have to worry. The essentials are complete. Everything can get started now."

Astel looked at her. "Zera, you are talking like a bad guy."

She smiled at him. "Am I? Oh, dear."

The gathered team members turned to watch as she was led outside by her boyfriend and off to the detention centre. She had planned for this, but that didn't mean she had to like it.

She was stripped out of her funeral clothes and com, put into loose scrubs, and hauled to a medical facility under guard.

Base scans and tissue samples were taken. Zera wasn't asked questions, so she didn't have to provide answers. She did as she was told as her psyche relaxed. The last week had been leading up to this moment, and now, she was relaxing and letting herself be removed by tiny pieces.

She was brought back to a cell, and she sat against the wall and let her brain think of absolutely nothing for a few hours. She slid down the wall and curled up on her bunk, falling asleep with remarkable ease. Her conscience was clear, and her agenda was open. The rest of her life was going to start as soon as she got out of there. It would involve a little more public exposure, but she had never been afraid to show off.

"Researcher Zera, you are here in front of this tribunal to answer the charges of wanton and premeditated murder."

She stood with her hands behind her back, and she lifted her head. "Six-zero-four-two-nine-seven-six. I am a registered bounty hunter with the state. The ashes were the remains of Mentor, and the doll maker is deactivated. Both were legal kills under the current program and peacekeeper guidelines for dealing with activated criminals."

They looked at each other, and one of them typed in the number. She sat back and whistled. "She is a registered bounty hunter for activated criminals. She registered this capture a week ago. Wait, why didn't we see this until now?"

Zera chuckled. "It only becomes visible with the number. Otherwise, you have to check under the nickname Hopper."

The tribunal looked at her, and one of the men drummed his fingers on the desk. "This was a revenge killing."

"It was removing a dangerous active from the general population before he killed more people. My sister may have been the catalyst to action, but she was not the initial issue that caused the bounty on their heads. There were other members of their organization that are still at large. You may want to look into them."

She waited for half an hour while the other info was checked and verified. Her registration had been a joke between her and Dainty. It was an in-case-of-emergency registration. If one of the patrons got out of hand, she needed to be able to take them down. It was not information that she shared with the patrons.

She stood and occasionally made minor shifts to her shoulders.

One of the tribunals frowned. "Are the cuffs too tight?"

"No. I am used to them."

"Do you get arrested a lot?" The female gave her a slight smile.

"No, mostly recreational confinement."

The tribunal froze.

"So, it is true that you are an escort?" one of the men asked her.

"Of course. I had to get the authorization, the legal precedent set, and the right to service actives to ease the psychosis caused by lack of physical contact. Contact with me also offers power-boosting benefits that are reaping rewards for those that they save."

The woman blinked and leaned forward. "What?"

"It is a fact that is on record. It is one of the reasons that Torun went from mid-range to team leader in a few months. He had more emotional equilibrium and was stronger, faster, and healthier. That is my active evolution. That and being able to hop in and out of the bodies of the willing. Sometimes, I can bring knowledge of how to use their active evolution with me."

The shock on their faces made her smile. They started quizzing her, and she answered their questions for an hour. When they were finished, they said they would review her case and let her know their decision.

Zera was led out of the meeting room and past Torun. "You're up, scooter."

He smiled and shook his head. "That's a good look for you. No bra?"

"Nope."

Her guards were upset by the flirting, but they hauled her back to her cell.

She was in her cell for two hours, having a cup of coffee, when a figure filled the hall outside the cell.

"Hey, Zera. The researchers would like to see you in action."

She grinned. "Why, Torun, I have no idea what you are talking about."

"Fine. They want to see *us* in action. In the lab. On the record."

"That's pretty pervy. Why ever would they want that?"

"To see if you do what you said you do." Torun grinned. "I have no objection."

"You just want to fuck on camera. I know it is one of your fantasies."

He shrugged. "So, humour me. My birthday is coming up." He gave her a charming smile.

"So, just so we have ground rules, what do you want to do?"

"I thought we could start on the exam table and see where we go from there. Maybe you can cut loose a little."

Zera smiled slowly. "How much?"

His eyes were glowing. "How much am I allowed to cut loose myself?"

"Well, these are your people, so it's up to you what you show them. I am good with whatever."

He nodded and unlocked her cell. "Hands for cuffs."

She turned and presented her hands for the cuffs. He pressed them in tight, and she went on her toes as her body started to throb in anticipation.

He whispered in her ear, "Don't get too hot too fast. They need a baseline."

"Then don't tighten the cuffs like that."

"But I like them like that." He chuckled.

"Yeah, that's the problem." She smiled. "Fine. You have to steer. I have been using this as a micro vacation, so I have no idea where we are."

He grabbed her by her arm and directed her down the hall. "This is not how I want this to go."

"I know, but I already have the all-clear for the killings. This is just because I have undisclosed activations. They want to see if I really do what I said I do."

"Oh, the boosting?"

"Yeah. This isn't just a chance for you to show off. I get to show off, too."

He chuckled. "They will be blinded by your beauty."

"Uh-huh. I don't think it is my beauty that they will be

watching. Something tells me that there is going to be a monitor of some kind inside my vag."

"I am sure they won't do that."

She looked at him sideways. "Oh, you sweet, innocent child. Researchers are ruthless bastards. I know. I am one."

They walked to the lab, and the folks in the coats were excited. "She agreed?"

Zera nodded. "She did. What do you need for a baseline?"

They had an array of monitor stick-ons and one internal probe. She looked at Torun, "See? Told ya."

He grinned. "Be quiet, and let them tell you what to do."

"Um, Team Leader Torun, we need her uncuffed for the baselines."

He murmured, "Behave."

"You aren't the boss of me."

His eyes narrowed. "Say that again when you finish the scans."

She grinned. "Don't tease."

The researchers were nervous as they started running scans, attached the monitors, and checked the feedback they were getting from it. The probe was thin, but it was attached to her, and it was about to get a workout.

Torun underwent a round of scans, and he was fitted with monitors as well. They were put in an observation room, and she turned to look at him. "Uh, researchers, I am gonna need some more clothes."

He hadn't bothered getting dressed after the monitors were put in place, and he definitely wanted to get started.

She looked into Torun's eyes, and he growled at her. She held up her hands. "Now, Torun, it hasn't been that long."

"Long enough. You worried me, Zera." He stalked toward her, and she backed up against the med bed. He lifted her and set her on the bed and grabbed her wrists, she heard and felt the clicks, and she was shackled to the bed in a semi-reclining position.

He threaded his hand in her hair, made a fist, and kissed her. "I believe I need an apology for worrying me."

She inwardly laughed her ass off but outwardly said, "I am sorry for worrying you, sir."

He bit her lip, and she turned serious as energy started humming in her veins.

Zera leaned up to him and met his tongue, stroke for stroke. When his hands came to the front of her shirt, she was unsurprised when the next sound was a wet tear. He dragged his lips over her neck, carefully supporting her head. He had to go around the monitor tabs on her chest but eventually got down to her breasts, where he nuzzled and licked at her skin. She whined gently as he nipped at her and muttered, "They don't need to see all the foreplay."

He lifted his head with his eyes gleaming. "They don't?" He slid his hand down her belly and stroked the slick heat of her sex. "Ah, they don't." Torun lifted her hips off the exam table and slid the scrubs off, and her slippers fell with them.

He made a deep humming sound in his throat as he stepped in between her thighs, gripping her beneath one knee as he fitted himself to her. The first thrust made her flinch, but the second filled her body with pleasurable fire. She looked up at him, and he smiled. "Just like old times."

She huffed. "You were a lot less cocky then."

He withdrew and went deep. "I was afraid of hurting you."

"That fear has passed?"

He chuckled. "That fear has passed."

She draped her free leg around his hips. "Then, get to it."

He kept a hand supporting her back, another holding her thigh, and he started to drive into her in earnest. He thudded into her hard; the wet sounds of bodies slapping punctuated their groans and the high sighs. She tensed and shrieked as she came. His body continued to hammer at hers until he grinned, and then, he withdrew and flipped her over.

She heard him murmur, "I bet they didn't put a probe in here."

She winced as he slid into her ass and wound a hand in her hair, pulling her head back and causing a wave of tension that caused her to constrict around him. He felt even larger in her ass, and she struggled against him, causing the roar and flex inside her. She felt the spurt inside her, and he moved slowly as he was undoing her manacles.

He kissed the back of her neck and licked at the sweat. "I wonder what they will make of that."

She sighed and pushed up against the med bed. "Well, since you are still inside me, I think they are still collecting data."

He kept moving inside her and reached around her to stroke her clit. "In that case, you should give them something more to analyze."

She dug her hands into the padding of the bed, and as she got closer to the edge, fabric tore and metal bent. She groaned as he guided her to the edge, held her there, and then tipped her over. She shouted, and the bed under her buckled.

"Aw, little tense, were we, pet?"

She shuddered as he pulled out of her ass, and she was held up by his arms around her. She gasped when he kissed her neck and started to lick slowly. "We aren't on our own, and I think the researchers have seen what they needed to. I just want to get dressed and get back to my cell while I wait for the results of the tribunal."

His hands tightened on her. "I want you to stay."

"You always want me to stay. We both need to go."

"I have nowhere I have to be."

She snorted as he nuzzled her neck and continued the slow licking. "Right, neither of us are getting together unless there is a shower in between and a few less monitor pods."

"Spoilsport."

"Well, since your *sport* involves two balls and a stick, yeah, I am a spoilsport."

"Ah, but I do love getting it in goal and going for extra points." He chuckled next to her ear.

A knock at the door got their attention. An abashed intern said, "There is a shower available, and Researcher Zera, here are some clothes."

It took a certain amount of balls to walk into a room with two naked actives. The intern put the clothing down on the table near the door and escaped.

Zera dropped the shreds of her top and started removing monitors. The first one to go was the slender one inside her. She set it on the table, and then, purple hands started to take the rest of them off her.

She murmured, "Shower now and play later, sir."

He laughed and left the room.

She groaned and stretched as she got the last of the pods off. The interior com opened. "Miss Zera, there is a small shower in the corner where you can clean up."

"Um, why? I can just shower and get dressed."

The voice was embarrassed. "He told us that if you weren't naked and waiting when he got back, he would try it with us."

She laughed and took the cool shower before drying off and hearing the door open and close. When she saw that it was definitely Torun, she jumped into his arms with her legs around his waist. "Hey, baby."

He chuckled. "Naughty little miss. What have you been doing since I have been gone?"

"In the last five minutes? Just scrubbing up."

"Are you clean now?"

She wrinkled her nose. "Mostly."

"Excellent. Me too. Hold on."

He slid into her and fucked her standing up. The

observers were making notes on the other side of the glass, and she blew them a kiss right before she gasped as the first release hit her.

The observers were in for a varied and detailed show.

# Chapter Eighteen

Zera was carried back to her cell and tenderly tucked in by a smug Torun.

"You cheated," was all she could mumble.

"They had to get their data. I was just giving them a large sample." He grinned.

"We took the monitors off."

"The room was rigged with sensors."

She stuck her tongue out at him; her body hummed with satisfaction. She chuckled. "We totally destroyed that room."

"We did."

"Did they mention their conclusions to you?"

"You are chatty when you are exhausted. I didn't know."

She snorted. "You are rarely around when I am coming down."

"Ah, I have reason to believe that that will change."

She was suddenly awake. "What?"

"The tribunal is taking the findings of our interactions into account, and they wish to keep you protected. Since there is no one better than me for that, they are looking at putting you under a version of protected arrest."

"For how long?"

"Until you cease being useful to the program."

She sat up. "What? No fucking way."

"That is what they have said."

"Delightful. They are about to find themselves out of all kinds of tech."

He frowned. "What?"

"Do you remember my day job as a researcher? All the

tech that the teams wear? All the non-lethal weapons and tech that the peacekeepers wear? That is all me. I have gotten all of the major supply contracts over the last five years. My companies design them all. It would be a shame if I became less than creative or shut down those branches of Z-Tech."

He smiled. "You would do that, wouldn't you?"

"Of course. You know me well. Hell, you know me best of all, but I do not like being hounded, pursued, or cornered. They will not put me under house arrest for the rest of my life and whore me out when they want to give one of their actives a boost. I decide. Legit citizen here. Some of the actives are just jackasses, and I don't want them near me or any of my team. Power does not make someone a good person."

"I know, Zera, but think about it. We could be together."

She wrinkled her nose. "I would love that, but you are on an international team, and if I am locked to you, where do I go when you are out of town. Into a box? Into a cell? I am a free citizen of this state. I have the rights of a citizen. I am a registered body-hopping active. No one bothered to ask what happened after I did that."

He chuckled. "You acquired your copying skills."

"Yes. I went into a body and came out with the copy activation."

"Who was it?"

She chuckled. "He's dead now, so don't worry about it."

"Vencorin."

"Yeah. Did you meet?"

"Yes, but he wasn't quite the same style of copycat that you are."

She shrugged. "I am one of a kind."

"Yes, sweet. You are, now get some rest. The tribunal is going to speak with you when you are a little less—"

"Sticky?"

He grinned. "We took a shower, remember?"

She hummed happily. "Oh, yeah. That is where I got sticky again."

He kissed her head. "Sleep, you naughty creature."

She grinned and laughed. "Bossy, sir."

"You know it."

He eased her flat and made sure she was covered before he left. She watched him go and surrendered to warm, achy sleep.

She was given a team suit to dress in for the verdict. She was wearing purple and black and had a feeling that it was significant. It had a low-keyhole neckline and a high collar. She ruffled her fingers through her hair and extended her hands for cuffs. The embarrassed keeper shook his head. "They are not necessary today, researcher."

She raised her brows and nodded. "Fair enough. Shall we?"

He nodded, and there was a blush in his cheeks. They were walking the hall, and he kept looking at her.

"Somewhere on a security monitor, there is porn starring Torun and me, right?"

"Uh, yeah. I haven't seen actives having sex before. Your eyes glow."

"Oh, yeah. That is a power-restraint thing. You are a peacekeeper?"

"Yes, Ma'am."

"Well, there is way more un-active porn out there than you can imagine. Why so impressed by a little connection?"

"You crushed the table, researcher."

"It's hard to be that wild and not touch your partner, but to do that, you need to keep control of yourself. The cuffs stop me from going too crazy too soon, but once they come off, I am allowed to go a little crazy. Pleasure is always a fun pastime. With a partner you trust, anything goes."

"Do you have any pointers?"

"Ease into things. Never go too fast, and if you want to

flirt with an active, tell them that you like their personality. They get comments about bodies and heroism all the time. They need to know that someone likes their laugh, the way they hold a cup, the tilt of their head while they are thinking. The things that give an insight into their personality. That is how Torun seduced me, and I told him I really liked purple."

He chuckled in surprise. "That was bold."

"He thought so. We went for ice cream and talked. Stick to public venues if they like, but avoid places they can strand you until you trust them."

His eyes widened. "Right. Good point."

Instead of going to the chamber, they were heading to one of the greater halls. "Where are we going?"

"There were those who requested permission to witness the tribunal's decision. There are several team members, a few corporate heads, and a governor's security detail complete with a governor."

She felt heat creep into her cheeks. "Ah, I had forgotten about her."

"So, you are bisexual?"

She shrugged. "People need affection, attention, and touch. Gender or sexual preference only chooses where it is most readily available. You can seek pleasure from anyone that you trust, and those aspects will grow. I care about the people. Their bodies are just the housings for their personality. I am more omnisexual than anything else. I will screw any shape of sentient being with a good personality."

"So, personality matters?"

They rounded a corner, and the entryway was lined with familiar faces, male and female, who nodded politely and blocked the reporters who were pushing and trying to get in for a better look at her.

She muttered to her escort, "Now I understand the suit."

He grinned, and they walked the channel to the tribunal

hall where every seat was taken up with her patrons, the patrons of other escorts, and a few of her friends. Khytten and Salat were standing together in a corner, his arms around her protectively.

Khytten was dressed neck to toe in black leather, and Salat was wearing matte black. They were an adorable couple. Zera smiled and waved at Khytten, Khytten waved back. Salat leaned and spoke in her ear, and Khytten blushed.

Zera grinned and walked up to the spot set aside for her. She had passed half a dozen figures wearing deep hoods with gleaming masks under them. Her employees had shown up for the event.

She faced the tribunal, and the men and woman were looking flustered. It was probably due to the dead silence in the space. No one was speaking.

The spokeswoman spoke, "Researcher Zera, while our teams would like to continue examining you and your skills, we understand that your importance to our community and those of neighboring countries is something that cannot be disregarded. We ask that you resume your normal activities and report in on a weekly basis to be monitored and scanned."

Zera smiled. "No. I do not have a condition that requires monitoring. I am stable, and it is the program's refusal to accept that an active can have cumulative aspects that has gotten us here today. That, and the legal termination of two know criminals."

"Ah, right. We have issued you the bounty for those two men and that portion of the case is closed."

"So, we are dealing with me, then?"

"Correct."

"May I address the assembled?"

The tribunal shrugged. The speaker said, "Please."

Zera raised her voice. "Who is here due to Z-Tech?"

About twenty persons stood up.

"Now, who is here due to the Blind Date Corporation?"

Close to a hundred of the assembled stood.

"So, these are the people who will be affected by what you say next. If I am turned into a lab rat, I will simply fold up all shops, discontinue all energy research, and disband the Blind Date Corporation, which up until this point had a plan for an entertainment venue at Uklanda Beach."

That had a murmur of interest through the room. It was two countries over, but the beach was legendary for its peace, tranquility, and nightlife.

Once the room was quiet, the spokeswoman said, "You would hold this stuff hostage?"

She grinned. "Of course not. I would kill it completely and salt the earth where these programs had been. Do not look so shocked. If you had been doing your job, helping those in need, passing exams, and creating useful tech all your adult life, and then someone says that *now we want to supervise you at all times*, you might get a little irritated. If you have been sharing your body and the boosting effect for years, you might get mad at the governing body that wants to flip the script and whore you out to the team members they think deserve a boost. I am a woman with choice, free will, and the ability to choose who I share with, and I choose carefully."

Zera smiled. "So, I either go free right now, or I don't, but the programs will come to a screeching halt if I don't leave here when this chat is over."

The tribunal looked down at their reports, and then, the gathered folks started radiating hostility.

One of the men spoke, "We can just start the escort program up ourselves."

"Can you? Can you match emotional needs as well as physical? Can you find the one person hiding in the population who has a desperate need but a powerful talent? Can you gain their confidence and promise them anonymity? When they freak out at the first date, will you hold their hand, give them a briefing? Will you teach them how to relax when their instincts are screaming at them to run because their date could tear them in half? Will you check on them after the date when they are wracked with guilt and panic? Helping them into the mood to return to reality after a night with the patrons is what I do. I help them straddle the two worlds, as do some other staff members. These men and women have lives. They are not to be locked in a box and pulled out for a quick lay and then stuffed back in. Some of them might even have partners if they can try enough people on for size."

The spokesperson frowned. "The teams can't have partners."

"No, but their partners can. That is the thing. The rules crafted are very one-sided. I am not a fan. So, the true setup is that they can't acknowledge their partners. That's fair enough. That is what the masks are for."

There were chuckles in the room, and the tribunal looked around. "There are some of them in here."

Zera nodded. "Both masked and unmasked."

Khytten called out. "Any questions?"

The tribunal stared at her ensconced in Salat's arms, and his expression told them to tread carefully.

"Uh, Miss . . ."

Salat grinned and growled. "She's my kitten. Address her as such."

The room at large chuckled, and Khytten lifted her arm and slammed her elbow back into Salat hard enough to make him exhale with a whoosh. She said, "Kitten is fine."

The team members froze, and the escorts chuckled.

"Um, Miss Kitten, how long have you worked in this capacity?"

"Eight months."

"How many interactions did you have in that time?"

"Three." Salat nudged her. "Six. Three individuals and then one persistent repeater. Three formally arranged dates. I am now on an exclusive contract."

The male on the left said, "I thought it would be more. You are a very attractive woman."

Khytten snickered. "I am suited for a niche market. My active adaptation means that I am either very attractive or completely repulsive depending on my partner's preferences."

"What is your active situation?"

She grinned. "None of your fucking business. Odds are it would be trial and error, but Zera kept folks from going after me as a novelty. The two other guys I met up with were nice, but there were no sparks beyond the obvious."

Salat murmured, "And as for her being for a niche market, I like her niche very much."

Laughter rippled through the room. Khytten looked resigned.

Salat continued. "Fortunately, there are no restrictions against actives mating and breeding in Aksalla. We do not have any trouble with folk attacking our families. They know better than to bring in civilians or to risk being eradicated with extreme slowness."

Zera was amused as Khytten's eyes bugged out. Apparently, they hadn't had that conversation yet.

"So, you are his romantic partner?"

Khytten blinked. "Um, yes, but he still has to book me."

Salat grinned. "A bargain at twice the price."

"You . . . he still has to pay?" The woman was surprised.

"Sure. I still have bills. Housing, that kind of thing."

"Oh, my god, you are the milkmaid." The woman blinked. "I saw your file . . . you . . ." She blinked. "Your name is actually Khytten."

Khytten wrinkled her nose. "Yes, and don't call me the milkmaid unless you want a solid punch to the nose."

Zera grinned. Khytten was armed to the teeth, and she was a superior shot. Sharpshooting might have been her second active category when she should have only had the one.

The tribunal looked at each other and brought up Khytten's file based on their next question.

"How will you deal with your partner being a citizen of a country you are banned from?"

Khytten snorted. "First, that is in the future, and second, we don't need to live in the same place to spend time together. We don't now, so I don't foresee an issue."

Salat growled. "It will be sorted." He tightened his arms around his kitten until she squeaked.

Zera smiled. "They are the first solid match that the Blind Date Corporation has created."

"What about you and Torun?" The man on the left spoke.

"Our match created the Blind Date Corporation and the legislation that lets the team members pay for escorts." She smiled. "Once that was in order, we could date in public with the auspices of the law on our side. Of course, given my nature, I welcomed other patrons, but Torun still gets to go first when he is available."

Tycho chuckled. "And sometimes we make group arrangements."

There was a combination of nervous laughter and knowing chuckles. The tribunal looked at each other and shrugged.

A gavel banged, and the speaker said, "As regards to the dispensation of Researcher Zera, we find that there are no grounds to hold her, and she may resume her normal activities in her various businesses. The findings of this tribunal are that she is of more use to her country in her standard capacity than as a research subject. She is free to go but is requested to answer a questionnaire as to her status with medical reports every six months. Is that acceptable, Zera?"

"It is. You have my contact information, so if you don't mind, I have somewhere to be this evening. I would like the return of my com if you could manage it."

One of the peacekeepers came up and handed her the com. She put it on her wrist. "Any luck decrypting it?"

The female in the tribunal snorted. "No. Whoever did your security is a monster."

Zera laughed. "Yeah, she is."

"Why isn't she working with the government?"

"She doesn't like peacekeepers." Zera smiled. "Also, she is another person whose interests became a secondary activation."

The tribunal looked at her. The man on the left said, "Do you have her name?"

"She's here in this room. Ask her yourself. As for me, I am on my way out. Have a pleasant day."

She left, and the room emptied out behind her, silent footfalls of those who found her useful created the feeling of a gathering storm. They exited the room, and the gathering outside encapsulated her while leading her to one of the team vehicles.

Tycho got behind the controls, and Ryma took the passenger seat, while Torun sat next to Zera in the back. "Where do you want to go, Zera?"

"I need to head to the research building. There is a project I have to attend to."

Torun raised his brows. "I thought we could celebrate."

She snorted. "We celebrated yesterday in front of the researchers."

"I thought we could celebrate as a team."

"As soon as I check on this project." She took his hand and squeezed it. "This is really important to me."

Tycho was already driving. "To the research centre we go."

She paused and then said, "Wait. Take us to Blind Date Corporation. That way, we won't need to use a portal."

Ryma asked, "We were going to use a portal?"

"Yeah, but out of everybody who was in that room, this is the group I trust with what I am going to show you."

She gave them the coordinates, and Tycho headed for her building. Now that they knew she was the owner of Z-Tech, things made a lot more sense, she could tell. Tycho's next words confirmed it. "I know you were a developer for the peacekeepers and the teams, but when did you open Z-Tech?"

"When I was fourteen. Susara's parents were killed shortly afterward." She sighed. "That is what started all this."

They pulled up in front of the building, and she got out, squared her shoulders, and headed for the main entrance. The team was behind her, and they went through the lobby, nodding to security on their way to the executive lift.

It was funny to have them all in the lift. "This is the tightest fit I have ever had with you three."

They chuckled, and Torun pulled her against him. "Why are we going down?"

"Because I picked this location perfectly. A secure spot was needed." They went down sixty feet, and then, the doors opened to Zera's private lab.

# Chapter Nineteen

"Holy gods." Tycho stared as they exited, and some of the most exotic tech on the planet was laid out before them.

"Yeah, don't peak too soon." Zera went to a wall with a huge metal door and used her hand, eye, tongue, and vocal registry. "Time to wake up, Dainty."

The door clicked and slowly opened. The vault opened, and the team members behind her stared in shock at the tube and the two dozen recumbent beds with the bodies of Susara on them.

Torun asked, "Zera, what is this?"

"This is Dainty's true activation. She started to make copies of herself when she activated. They were living bodies but not awake or aware. It wasn't until she was killed with our parents that we understood what they were for. The oldest body got moving, but she was missing her memories, so I found a mind transfer active and hopped through them. After that day, I kissed her forehead and downloaded her mind once or twice a week."

Torun was staring. "I have seen you do that. So, Susara is alive?"

"She is. Her heart beats, her body moves, and I just have to give her her mind back. So, we are here today to get me my sister back."

Ryma looked around. "How many backups does she have?"

"Here, twenty-four. Around the world. A few more." She laughed. "Before you ask, they age as she ages."

"That is so odd." Tycho looked into one of the enclosed beds and looked at the empty shell. "Why couldn't you just upload her psyche into her empty body?"

"The connection between body and soul was broken. When the doll maker did his work, he shredded through memory engrams, shorted out nerves, and gave her a dying brain. There was no coming back from that."

She triggered the tank to flush the fluid that the body had been in, and when the body was curled on the empty grill, she had the tube rise.

"What are you doing?"

"Removing the electrodes that have been helping her with muscle tone. One time I had to do this, and she just flopped around for a week. So, now I have a series of electrodes that I put in, and it runs her body through an exercise regimen. She's still weak, but she will be able to walk with help." Zera went to a cupboard and pulled out an adorably soft blue suit with rigid struts in it.

Torun asked, "What is that?"

"It's a walking suit."

Tycho looked at it. "I have seen those in hospitals for paralyzed victims. They can get them up and around until a healer for their issues can be located. It keeps their organs healthy."

"And handles waste until muscle control can be regained." Zera set it down near the body that was sleeping peacefully.

She picked up her sister and carried her to a cleaning station, washing and drying her before setting her in a chair. Zera noticed that she had an audience. "Can I get some privacy?"

The team said, "No."

She snorted. "Fine, I guess I did invite you down here."

She sat next to Susara and leaned in, pressing a kiss to her forehead. She exhaled, and her mind expanded to let the backup of Susara flow into her. The data had already been updated by the machines. This was to restore her soul.

Susara was still for a moment, and then, her eyes moved, and her lashes fluttered open. "Zera! How long have I been gone?"

"Just over a week."

"How much time did I miss before upload?"

"Two days, including the day that you died."

"Aw, geez. I am so sorry. Hopper, why are there three team members looking at me?"

"It has been a helluva week. Oh, and all our stuff burned, except for what I put in storage. The house is gone."

"What? Damn. Is my suit ready?"

"Of course, bossy boots. It's good to have you back." She stroked the candy-coloured hair away from her sister's face. "I missed you."

Zera took a deep breath and continued the briefing, "Oh, the Blind Date Corporation had been exposed because of a mouthy purple jackass who shall not be named."

"Zera, I am right here."

She ignored him.

"How is the team?"

"They are good. We have lost Eleven as an escort. She's still on the books, but she has an exclusive contract."

"Wow, we can do that now?"

"Her patron insisted, and since she is specific, it seems right."

Torun chuckled. "If Zera could handle it, I would go for the exclusive immediately."

Zera smiled. "But then, he would have to stay home and spend hours satisfying me, and then, do it all over again the next day."

Dainty smiled and struggled into the bodysuit with Zera's help. When she was dressed, she asked, "Did we get him?"

"We got him. Mentor dead, doll maker dead and in pieces."

Dainty hugged her. "Did you see Delvis?"

Tycho said, "He was taken into custody."

"So, you didn't kill him?"

"No, if you want to, though, you aren't technically alive again yet."

Dainty giggled. "You have made improvements to the suit."

"Nothing is too good for my little sis."

Tycho asked, "Why do you call each other sisters? You are obviously not related."

Susara smiled. "She was there when I was born, she helped me with my first steps, and she went through school with me, held me when our parents died, and helped me train for the program. Ohmygod. Did we take the exam?"

Torun chuckled. "You did. You passed, top of your class. Zera passed, too, using analytical skills and surprising physical prowess."

Susara blinked. "What?"

"I wore him and punched my way out of a rubble pile."

"Nice."

Torun laughed. "It felt most peculiar. Like she was touching me from the inside."

"I got out of you as fast as I could."

He chuckled. "We have very different instincts. When I am inside you, I want to stay there as long as possible."

Susara got her suit sealed, and she wavered to her feet. Her eyes went wide, and she winced. "Right. So, the suit has attached."

Zera chuckled. "Great. Let's go break in your stomach."

She looked at the team. "Did you want to come? We are going up to the Blind Date headquarters."

They nodded. "We are at your service until we get a call, researcher."

"Right. Out of the vault and into the lift."

Susara smiled and let Zera help her as they left the vault with her bodies inside and the door locked up behind them. They headed to the lift, and Tycho asked, "If I am a very good boy, can you bring me back here and give me a tour?"

Zera held her sister up and gave the ocular scan for the

upper levels where Blind Date was located. They exited the lift, and once again, they looked like they had stumbled into a candy store.

Torun asked, "Does every escort have their own rooms?"

Zera nodded. "Of course. Makeup, bathing, and grooming facilities. The wardrobe tailored to that particular escort, it is all here."

She walked Susara to the kitchen area and looked at her companions. "Anyone hungry?"

Everybody agreed that they were hungry, and that was enough. Susara grinned. "Oh, this is gonna be good."

Zera started chopping, mincing, sauteing, and moving around the kitchen while noodles cooked and rice steamed. In half an hour, plates were slid in front of Susara and the team. "Susara eats first."

The team got the hint, and Zera brought out another round of fried dumplings and blazing hot dipping sauces. Susara liked heat.

The food-prep orgy stopped, and she put stuff in the washer before heading to the table. The sticks were all that she had provided, and the team wasn't nearly as dexterous as they should be for international travellers.

She took a few bites, and then, she turned to Torun. "Open."

He opened his mouth, and she dropped in a mouthful worth of stir fry.

He ate, and Tycho leaned forward and opened his mouth. She fed him and Ryma as well.

She got what she needed first and then helped them speed up their eating while Susara giggled.

Susa chuckled. "By the way, Zera, you and Torun totally look like a couple. I like that suit."

"Thanks. They gave it to me for the teams' tribunal today that decided whether I would be allowed to walk free."

Susa said, "What? Catch me up."

Torun grinned. "We had to have sex in front of

researchers for hours to prove her activation."

Susa frowned. "Wasn't that one of the top ten fantasies in your file, Torun?"

He blinked. "You read that?"

"Sure. She can't vet all that information on her own. I design the costumes tailored to the fantasy lists. Zera's extruders make the designs come to life. I had some great ones for Eleven, but I never got a chance to see them on her."

"I showed a few to her, and we just have to let her patron pick. I am sure he is going to go for the spring priestess outfit."

Susa smiled. "Nice, who is her patron?"

The team answered as one, "Salat."

Susa blinked. "Really? Wow. Oh, wait. The human milk-cream thing. Right. Makes sense."

Ryma asked. "You don't even comment on the compatibility issue elsewhere?"

Susa shook her head. "No, Eleven has all of the characteristics of a woman who has just given birth; she could fit a melon in there if she absolutely had to."

Torun sighed. "Ah, I am in mourning for a missed opportunity."

Zera smiled. "Try it with her now. I dare you."

His look was black. He wouldn't admit it, but Salat was more dangerous than he was. The projection blades he wielded could easily behead an opponent, and Torun would have to crush Salat before he got close enough to murder Torun. No one did well without a head.

Zera kept eating, and when she was finished, she waited until the team and Susa had their fill. She boxed everything into containers and put it in the fridge for any escorts who were peckish after their dates. There was an open-fridge policy.

As if summoned, Fifteen came into the space and froze. She had her mask dangling from her fingertips, and she blushed crimson in seconds. "Uh. Hi. Sorry, Zera, I just came in to get a drink before I get ready."

"It's fine. Sorry. We were just having a meal because Susara is back with us."

Susa grinned and waved. "Hello again. Rumours of my death were accurate. I am the backup of the backup of the backup. It's one of my activations."

"Well, I am just going to ease past you and grab a drink and then be on my way to my changeroom."

She eased past the team and grabbed a sports drink from the fridge. She then eased past them again, and Zera watched as Torun and Tycho were looking at their available escorts, and Fifteen wasn't on their listing.

Torun asked Zera, "Why can't I see her profile?"

"She isn't for you. She doesn't have physical resistance, she has mental resistance, and you don't need that." Susara sipped at the tea that Zera had made for her. "There are other patrons rather than the ones who can lift cars."

Zera nodded. "If either of you two got excited, you would tear right through her."

They looked appalled.

She shrugged. "This is why the matchmaking aspect of the corporation is important. Making sure that patrons match the escorts is vital."

They sat around discussing the plan to match patrons with acceptable escorts and vice versa.

Fifteen came through the lobby forty minutes later, and Zera walked over to speak quietly to her. Fifteen opened her cloak and showed the outfit of silk and lace. It was the sort of outfit a businessman would want his mistress to wear in public. Dignified but with the promise of sex. The four-inch heels sold the look.

"Have fun. Call if you need me."

"Thanks, Mom. I will be fine." She resettled her cloak, bowed to the team and Susara, and left via the lift, a security bot joining her in the elevator.

Zera sighed. "It's her first date with him. He is a little on the brusque side, but she should be fine. I worry about all of them when they go out, and I keep an ear out until they are all back with their security bots."

"The security bots. What do they do?" Tycho asked. "I have seen others with them, but they never do anything."

Zera snickered. "Susa, do you want to take this one?"

"Sure. Attach a security bot to my life signs."

Zera grinned and did it as Susara got to her feet. "Well, you are the best suited for it, so push me over, sis."

Zera picked her sister up, shook her, and then threw her to the floor. The security bot arrived at Susara's side and wrapped around the body on the floor. Susara stood upright in heavy armour and raised her hand to Zera. "Want me to blast you now or later?"

"We can skip the blasting, but this is what the security bots are. It keeps me safe while giving me the option to fight or run." Susara's voice came out of the bot.

The team members were fascinated by the bot armour.

Torun asked, "How many times has this been used?"

"Twice. Both times the active calmed the fuck down once pinned to the wall. They were removed from our roster and banned. The escort was offered and received counselling."

Ryma asked, "How was she? Was it a she?"

"Good guess, in this case, yes, it was a she. Her clients had strong prey drives, and they got violent when she did what she was contracted to do and acted like prey. She still works with us but now is nearly exclusively first dates. She helps us introduce the patrons to the protocols. She does it so that no one needs to use the security bots."

Tycho frowned. "Have I met her?"

"No, you were well entrenched with the escorts from the start. She prefers working with the new patrons. In case you think she is having sex with them, she usually isn't. This is a new protocol that we are instituting for patrons with general interests. The ones with specific escorts in mind have to wait."

Ryma smiled. "Like Salat."

"Yeah, he had something specific that he needed, and to everyone's shock, she turned up." Zera nodded. "We have a few more patrons like that on the books, so we wait until an escort shows up for them. Thanks to Torun running his mouth, we have a flurry of applications for escorts and patrons."

Susa laughed. "Good. I can get right back to the security checks and assigning monitoring to the patrons."

"And with the increase in business, you can decide whether you want to join a team or not, Dainty."

"Well, if I just passed, I have a few months to decide and look for a placement." Dainty grimaced. "I also have to find a team where I haven't had sex with any of the members, which is more difficult than it should be. I might join the family business after all."

She flexed. "I need a new com."

Zera nodded. "I have one for you. I also told the regen department that you would be returning to action. They will issue you your details when you show up and do the confirmations."

"Nice. Is there any record of my test? I want to know how you managed it."

Zera looked to Torun, and she smiled slightly. "I had to use your venom."

"Why are you looking at him?"

"He was part of the test. I had to use your Suit Bait draw and then subdue him. It was not a fun test."

Torun laughed. "It was for me. She used your venom to knock me out and shoved me at the team she was assigned, saying that they had a small window to cuff me and less time before I broke loose. You have a powerful weapon there."

"Yeah, but it is hard to administer. I have to know the subject's composition before I can make the toxin." Susa smiled. "Which, I don't really, so it was Zera's knowledge that knocked you on your ass."

Zera pulled the vids and put them on the screen. They watched the slender and trembling form that was Susa enter the warehouse and go about her business.

The kiss between Dainty and Torun did not look like a first kiss.

Torun asked Zera, "Can you do the same?"

"Yeah. I copied it when we were teens. I passed it along after Susa started getting targeted."

Tycho laughed. "You can pass on activities?"

"Sure. I just need an understanding of the active's manifestation. Venom is difficult and easy at the same time. It is chemistry and biology. It took me a while to get the hang of it, but once I developed the instinct for it, I passed it along." She smiled. "Well, now that dinner is over, I need to find a place for Susa and me to stay."

Torun smiled. "Stay with me."

Tycho and Ryma looked from Torun to Zera. Tycho said, "He does have a lot of room. We crash there a lot when we don't want to go back to our base."

Susa got up and hugged her. "It sounds like as safe a place to be as anything else. Come on, let's go."

Zera blinked. "You seriously want to go?"

"I want a nap, with sheets, a pillow, and I want to let myself settle into this body. You know how it goes."

"Fine. Whatever you want, Susa. I will pack some small bags for us. Back in a moment."

Ryma smiled. "Can I come look? I always wondered what your wardrobe was like."

"Sure. This way."

Zera led her into Susa's changing area. "Two has a fairly extensive wardrobe and hasn't used half of it. We need to get some comfortable items that she can rest and lounge in."

She typed in the criteria, and a selection of clothing was

sorted out and came toward her in an open closet. "We pick what we need for the evening. You guys are pretty good about making your decisions on what you want us to wear, and then, we put it on."

"This screen is a catalogue?"

"It is."

"Wow. Did you design all this?"

Zera brought up the underwear collection and packed the bag. "I did. When I was ten. I have been designing tech for a while, but that is what I was born to do, it seems. That and have a crush on Torun."

"A crush? You two are in love with each other."

"Yes." She smiled and finished the toiletry set. "Right, now let's do me."

"Oh, yes, let's." Ryma smiled.

They left Susa's changeroom and went into Zera's. Zera grabbed a bag, and she ordered her underwear first. Ryma eased in past her and made a few more lingerie selections before Zera snorted and got some business clothing as well as a bit of casual.

She included a few creams and her favourite shampoo and closed up the bag. "That's it. No more silliness."

Ryma hugged her. "I am so happy you are going to his place."

"Why?"

"You will see."

With that taunt, they joined the others and got in the lift to descend. It was about to get busy for the evening, so it was best that they didn't freak out the escorts. Not everyone was as calm as Fifteen.

# Chapter Twenty

He was still within range of summoning a transport by twenty feet. "That is pretty close."

Torun shrugged. "It was on your list."

Tycho and Ryma chuckled.

"My list?" Zera was confused.

Torun opened the main doors. "Six years ago, we were together, and I asked what it would take for you to move in with me. You went into detail, and you might have been a little drunk. This is the house that those ramblings created."

Susara caught on before Zera did. "You built her a house?"

"I had it built for her. I wanted a place we could meet that wasn't always a hotel or restaurant." He opened the door and invited them in.

Zera was the last to enter. She hesitated and stepped over the threshold and into his arms.

Tycho said, "I will take Susara to a guestroom. Where should I take Zera's bag?"

"Our room." He looked down at her and smiled.

She blinked. "Our room? We have a room?"

"And a very big bed for when Ryma and Tycho join us."

She chuckled. "You seem pretty confident that it is going to happen that way."

"You can get a transport. I have vehicles in the garage. Communications are easy, and I have a secure system ready for you to work from." He rubbed his hands over her back. "I have questions that I would like you to answer."

"Sure. What would you like to know?"

"I think we can take a quick tour, and then, we can talk

in the bedroom."

She sighed in disappointment. "You actually mean to talk. Fine. Show me your castle."

He kept an arm around her as he showed her the great room, the pool, games room, gym, kitchen, dining room, guestrooms, and finally, the main bedroom. There was a walk-in closet, and to her amusement, two adjoining bedrooms. Ryma's and Tycho's touches in the rooms were unmistakable.

"You guys puppy pile?"

"Not yet, but with you here, probably sooner rather than later." He smiled, and she caught the deeply happy glow in his eyes.

"What questions did you have?"

"Who was Mentor to you?"

She blinked. "What?"

"I put an audio tracker on your suit, and I heard you discussing things. It was a confusing conversation, and it left me with questions."

"I doubt you found it confusing."

"Indulge me. Who was he to you?"

Zera looked at her lover. "He was my brother. We shared the same birth species but no genetics. We arrived in a clutch about a hundred years ago, fell to earth from a seeding species, and we remained developing but mostly dormant until thirty years ago when a researcher found us and brushed against our eggs. That changed us into creatures who looked human. We hatched, and they had six children on their hands. One little girl and five little boys. All curious with aspects of power. We were taken to a research facility and kept in isolation until I saw a purple prince walking through the facility. I had to touch you, and when I did, I understood all of your potential."

She shrugged. "You were the prettiest thing I had ever seen, and to me, you still are. Convention being what it is, I had to wait until I was an adult, which meant I needed to grow. I had to learn how to shape myself with Mom's new baby. And when we were the same height, I started to age with her."

"So, you are something else." He frowned. "Something not human."

"I appear human on scans, and that is what matters. It is just assumed that my active status mutated me a little."

"What happened to the other four males?"

"I blew them up. They had started to age quickly and were eyeing the female researchers. When one of them made a move on Mom, I had to kill them all. They were getting really aggressive. With Mentor, it appears that I missed one. I made sure of it this time."

"What was their purpose?"

"To procreate and fill the world with offshoots of our kind."

"What was your purpose?"

She chuckled. "To rule them."

He stepped toward her. "That is a very natural state for you, isn't it?"

Zera wrinkled her nose. "It just seems to happen."

"What did you do to me? There was something different after I met you and for the next decade and a half."

"Ah, I took your killing rage, lover. I took it and held it until you were able to deal with it again." She smiled. "When I could give you a physical outlet, you could take the rage back and use it for your own benefit."

He stared at her for a minute, and her smile faded. "Did I say too much?"

Torun walked toward her and kissed her. "Are you saying that you use sex to calm me down?"

She shook her head. "No, it is strictly a form of appreciation for your efforts on behalf of the population. And fun. It is a helluva lot of fun."

He grinned. "Glad to hear it. You know what my next question is, don't you?"

"Maybe, but can we have sex first? I don't think I have really ever gotten to sleep the night through with you."

"You think I want to sleep the night through with a strange and mysterious alien?"

She blinked. Unsure. Suddenly, her heart hurt, and that didn't normally happen. She looked up at him, and her eyes filled with tears. "I guess not?"

She stepped away, and he caught her and held her against him. "You guessed wrong."

She kissed him with relief and stroked his cheeks, his neck, and ran her hands down the front of his suit. "I thought you wouldn't want me if you knew."

"I will always turn to you. You know that." He slid his fingers into the closure of her suit. "I do love you in purple."

"I do love purple in me." She smiled as the suit was opened, and he knelt to use his mouth on her breasts. She shivered and wove her fingers through his hair. She moaned and held him to her as his hands continued working her suit off. She had to lose her grip on him until she was naked from the waist up. Her body throbbed, her blood hummed, and she slowly moved to the closure of his suit. She exposed him inch by inch, and when the suit was open, she touched the warm skin and felt his pulse under the muscles of his chest.

She shuddered when he started to use his teeth and yelped as he playfully tugged on a nipple. "Wiseass."

He peeled out of his suit to the waist, and he pulled her against him, wrapping his arms around her and burying his head between her breasts. Zera inhaled the scent of him, and she said softly, "Have I thanked you properly for coming to support me today?"

"No thanks necessary. It was nice to be able to do something for you for a change." He smiled. "Aside from paying to train more escorts."

"You have been an amazing patron, Torun, and a better friend."

"Is it a good friendship or what the modern un-activateds call friends with benefits?"

"I will take the friendship and give you the benefits." She stroked his face softly.

He nodded. "I think we are overdressed."

"I would agree. If you let me go, I can do something about it."

"No, while you are under my roof, you will obey my rules. I get to undress you."

She shivered but blinked. "I don't know. Your rules usually end up with me tied up."

He chuckled. "I haven't shown you the playroom yet. That is where that sort of thing will take place." His fingers eased the suit off her hips.

"There is a whole room for it?"

"Certainly. It isn't the sort of thing Ryma would enjoy doing to you. Tycho said he would like to watch, and I need an outlet for those dark impulses, dear Zera."

She shivered. "Oh."

"I see you like the thought of being at my mercy."

She bit her lip and then said, "You don't have any mercy, sir."

"Ah, pet, you know just what to say. Step out."

She stepped out of the suit, and he took it, shook it out carefully, and hung it up. "You had it made for me."

He chuckled. "I have been keeping it for just such an occasion when my clear support could not be missed."

"Is it wired for sound and full of trackers?"

He grinned. "Yes. Now, where were we?"

"You were overdressed and promising me unspeakable torments."

He grinned. "That will wait; tonight, I want to see pleasure in your eyes."

She looked at him and cocked her head. "In that case . . . strip."

He laughed and pushed his suit off his hips before sitting

and yanking off his boots and the last of the fabric.

He reached for her, and she fell into his arms, locking him in a kiss that curled her toes and made him hold her tight.

Torun fell back and rolled with her until they were in the centre of the soft space. She was pinned under him, and he smiled, stroking her cheek and neck. "So very soft. Your eyes changed when you grew. The original green was striking."

She smiled. "I had to change it when I tried to be human. It was too striking for someone who was otherwise normally pigmented."

"And your skin was paler."

"Had to change that, too."

"And you used to be bald, but I like the hair." He chuckled.

"Thanks. It was particularly itchy when it grew in. Mom had to help me."

"You called her Mom?"

"Yeah. She was a mother, so I called her Mom, and when she had her baby, I called it sis, and together, we named her Susara."

"What happened to her husband?"

"He was injured in the blast with the five hatchlings. Well, four hatchlings. I missed one."

"You crippled him?"

She shrugged. "I was a child. My aim was sloppy. When I breathed the fire, I wasn't exact enough. He was understanding enough until Mentor killed them."

"You breathe fire?"

"Not anymore. That biological system has ceased to function."

"Aw, that would have been fun to see."

She wrinkled her nose. "Are we going to discuss my activation again?"

He grinned. "Intermittently. Can I tell the team what you

are?"

"Do you want to?"

"No. I would rather you be my secret. This is above their pay grade."

She smiled. "It will come out eventually. I am not done evolving yet."

"What do you think you were put here to do?"

"To start my race all over again with a dash of human bloodline. That is why the activity started to begin four hundred years ago. It was a primer."

He blinked. "Your species did that?"

"Yeah. It was what they needed to do to make suitable mates here. Three hundred years was enough time to disperse the activity. Then, we were dropped here, and you have already heard the rest."

"So, what I am hearing is that you are all alone on this world."

"Yes. I only have the friends and family I have collected."

He slid his body along hers, and she arched up and rubbed herself against all available planes and angles.

"So, I am all you have." His voice vibrated with energy.

"You are all I have; you are all I want." She slid her legs on either side of his thighs.

He reached between them and rubbed the head of his cock against her. "Oh, so ready."

He thrust in, and she inhaled and arched against him, gripping his shoulders. "Ohhh. Now I feel like I am home."

He kissed her. "So do I. Hang on." He withdrew nearly completely and then thrust in to the hilt.

She lifted into every plunge and slide; the friction of him moving inside her over and over drew moans and grunts that matched his as he propelled her toward orgasm. She started begging when her body would tense, and he slowed. He moved with her and kept her from sending herself over.

When she reached for herself, he grabbed her hand and pinned it to the bed, kissing her hard. "Now, now, no cheating."

She gasped and slid her tongue against his, licking at his lips and whimpering. His self-control had been her gift to him, and it was a torture to her. She flexed her fingers against his, and he held her while he pounded into her with a slow, inexorable beat.

Her orgasm burst free with a heavy pulse that throbbed through her limbs. She groaned as it went on and on with his continued forays inside her. Zera shuddered as her body gripped him tight, and his face took on his cruel smile. "Oh, poor thing, it just goes on and on for you."

She squirmed and tried to get out from under him, her body getting more sensitive by the moment. She spoke in a soft and breathy tone. "Please."

"What is that now?"

"Please stop, sir. Or cum. Please cum, sir."

He grinned. "You will have to do better than that."

"Please, sir, I want you to cum inside me. I want the chance that I can have your child. Only you, sir. I only want your offspring."

His eyes blazed. "Can you?"

"Yes, it isn't easy, and it will take a very long time, but I am made for it. I will have—oh!"

He thrust into her and shuddered as he groaned, and he threw his head back, his neck corded with effort. She felt the spasms inside and smiled in relief as he stopped moving.

Zera held him as he slowly collapsed on her. She stroked her fingers through his hair and pressed soft kisses to his temple. "You are my mate. No matter who I sleep with, you are the one I turn to, every time."

He lifted his head and looked down at her. "You are my mate. You can escort five hundred patrons, and I will be there waiting to take you in my arms. You can ease their pain, loneliness, suffering, and help them find themselves again, and I will wait to hold you through the night when I can."

"I want to reduce my active role at Blind Date once I have more personnel, more branches. I like the choosing, the coaching. I like helping folks find the right fit for a night or longer."

There was a pause. "Can you really have my child?"

"Yes. As I said, it will take some time. My implant shorts out in four months. I will need a secure bunker in six months, or I will have to keep the incubator at my new house. You are not going to burn that one down, are you?"

He blinked at her in surprise. "Whatever could you mean?"

"I mean, you have been trying to coax me into moving in with you for a few months, and you didn't like me being alone when Susa died, so you did what you thought was appropriate. You took my house off the table. It wasn't safe, there was no one sharing it with me, and you had somewhere you wanted to put me. You burned down my fucking house."

He sighed. "Are you going to report me?"

"No, but I still need a property of my own."

"Why? You can live here."

"I can, and I intend to, but I need a place halfway between here and the city for work purposes. Meeting with escorts and doing design sessions with Susa. Plus, Susa might not be comfortable living here. She might look around and join a team, but she needs a place to call home. All her life has been with me, so I want to stay close until she doesn't need me anymore."

He smiled. "But, you want to stay with me?"

"I do. I always have. I think we are wearing them down." She chuckled and flexed her fingers against his.

He grinned, kissed her, and started moving inside her again. "Well, in that case, I am practicing."

"What?"

"Getting you pregnant. Will you lay an egg?"

"I have no idea. I do know that I have created an incubator that has been used successfully in a few experiments. Technically, I won't have your child; I will incubate it. Hell, I don't know if I lay eggs or not."

He chuckled. "As long as you call me your mate, I don't care if you give birth to a bright purple squid."

She grinned. "That could definitely be an interesting team member."

He rocked inside her slowly, kissing her softly. It was the sweetest coupling that she could remember, and when she came, he was with her. It was definitely a good practice run. They would make excellently weird parents . . . eventually.

They spent hours with each other and cuddled up in each other's arms. She followed what he had told her earlier and whispered, "Open doors."

It took three minutes before they were in a cuddle pile with Ryma and Tycho on either side of her and Torun watching over all three of them. They simply held each other and slept. It was an excellent way to enjoy the first night in a house, surrounded by people she trusted.

Susa carried a tray full of coffees and pastries in at dawn. She grinned as she set it down and brought the cup over to the bed. A pale limb came out of the pile as Zera fought her way out of the stack of heroes and took the coffee. "Thanks, Susa."

Zera yawned. "I would go for a run, but my legs are currently being used as pillows."

Susa laughed. "I can skip a few runs. You look happy."

"I am. While I was stuck, I had some more ideas for Khytten's birthday party."

"Are you throwing a party?"

"I am. Salat's orders. He wants his kitten to have a party, so she will have a party." She chuckled. "I have a few ideas about a theme. We are inviting all the escorts who want to come and a few select patrons."

Torun looked up from his spot, belly down in the sheets. "Are we invited?"

"If you are available, of course. All three of you. Dress will be formalish, though."

Ryma looked up. "What is formalish?"

"Fancy with a lot of bare skin."

Susa laughed. "I can help with clothing."

Zera slugged down her coffee. "Good idea, Susa. We will just provide the clothing, and guests can change when they arrive. It will make things more uniform."

Susa nodded. "All escorts will be invited?"

"Yup."

"Excellent. I have a ton of designs I never got made up. I can totally make up a few dozen in different colours for both genders. If I can get a tablet, I can start having the CAM units get underway."

Zera finished her coffee, and Susa grabbed the mug. Ryma looked at her with sleepy eyes. "Are you getting up now?"

Susa laughed and left the room.

Zera flopped back, and the team started to move around her. She was soon pleasurably swamped under muscled limbs and had to admit it was a nice way to start the day.

# Epilogue

Zera spent a few days setting things in motion and interviewing new escorts. She managed to get five in process, and twenty-three new patrons were running through security checks.

Khytten called her every day to ask her to cancel the party. Each time, Salat's com cut in, and he stated that the party would continue. The two other patrons that had had Khytten in their arms were also invited.

With the party taking place that evening, Susa was back in the swing of things, legal and registered with her working com.

At the venue, she organized the caterers, the decorations, and the racks of itemized costumes for the event.

This was the first big party that they had engaged in. There would be alcohol available for those who wanted it, but anyone stepping out of line would be dealt with.

With twenty minutes before the first guest was to arrive, the birthday girl showed up with her backpack on. Mortified.

"We still have enough time to cancel this, Zera. I am really not good with folks staring at me."

"Khytten, there are times in life when a little attention is warranted. Birthdays are one of those times. Come on, Salat wanted you to have this party, and I want to throw it, so all you have to do is enjoy it."

Khytten groaned. "No fair bringing him up. He has to work tonight."

Zera gave her friend a hug. "There will be plenty of friends and familiar faces here tonight, but first, we have to get you dressed."

"This is going to be embarrassing, isn't it?"

"Yup, but don't worry. We are all playing dress-up tonight. Even the patrons."

Khytten grumbled but allowed herself to be dressed in a heavily modified outfit consisting of a skirt, a top, and a cape, all designed to show as much as possible.

Zera was in something similar, but instead of Khytten's green, Zera was wearing black and purple. Susa put on some pastel blue, and the other escorts arrived and got dressed. Several brought gifts for the birthday girl.

It was another hour before the patrons showed up, and the escorts smiled as the patrons showed up wearing less than they were for a change.

Zera mingled with the guests as they paid their respects and gave well wishes to Khytten.

Music started, people danced, and Khytten refused to dance with anyone. Zera watched and sighed. Her friend was unhappy and lonely, even in a room full of people.

Presents flowed toward her, and she started to open a bunch of presents, mostly scents and grooming items. Fifteen gave her a beautiful shawl with butterflies patterned and swirling on it. When it was Zera's turn, she carried the case to Khytten and presented it. The birthday girl opened the box and stared. "Oh, wow. Is this really for me?"

"It is. They are all your weapons. Fully adjustable from stun to cutting through steel. Don't get those two mixed up." Zera explained the cuffs and what they could do. "Do not think of testing them out right now."

Khytten grinned. "I won't, but I have no idea how I am getting this home. I came on my cycle."

"We will have your presents delivered. I am sure Salat can arrange it."

"Sure. Tomorrow when he gets home."

Khytten paused when she felt something familiar. Hands caressed her shoulders from behind her chair. She looked and only saw the slight pressure marks on her arms.

"If you want me to wait until tomorrow to celebrate your birthday, you are mistaken." His low, smooth voice rolled over her.

"Ooh, Salat. You made it." She smiled.

"Yes, kitten. Would you like to dance?"

"I don't know how. I practiced with projections like I was taught, but I have never done it with another person."

His lips touched her ear. "I can help you with that. I don't mind if you step on me, kitten. You look lovely."

He touched her hand. "Come on. I won't let you fall."

She turned her fingers in his and looked to where his face was. "Promise?"

"Promise."

He tugged her to her feet, and she clung to his arm, noticing. "What are you wearing?"

"The same as most of the other patrons here."

Her eyes went wide as the men were wearing short skirts and not a lot else. She blinked. "Can I see?"

"Yes, kitten."

He led them to the dancing area and turned in her arms. He became visible, and she looked down at the soft black hip wrap that fell just past mid-thigh. "Oooh, best present ever."

"I am not your present, kitten." He pulled her toward him, and his skin made contact with her bare abdomen, and she held tight to him as he started to sway with her.

"I have never understood why people get a prize for getting older."

He smiled at her, his hair neatly braided along his scalp, making his pointed ears stand out. "You deserve a prize for surviving and getting this far."

"I am still thinking that present is you, Patron. How did you get here so fast?"

"Airlift to the building. Zera thoughtfully chose one with a landing pad."

She blushed. "Oh. You shouldn't have hurried."

"And miss my kitten's birthday? Never. I would have gone faster if I could."

She smiled. "It wasn't necessary. Usually, the day comes and goes without comment."

They moved together and twirled around and around. He turned her, dipped her, and she clutched him in panic. He kissed her, and the world fell away.

"Ah, Salat. I have missed you. Four days gone and only the occasional growl in my ear."

He smiled. "It is my version of letting you know I am still alive."

"Well, it did do that."

He leaned in and murmured, "And I like what you do when you hear my voice."

She blinked. "You can hear that? I am going to need better sound protection."

"Trying to deprive me of the little soft sounds is a punishable offense, kitten."

"Why?"

"What did the contract say about privacy?"

"Um, it is at your discretion."

"And when it involves listening in to your pleasure, I choose to hear it all."

Khytten felt the fullness in her breasts, and she blinked. "I need to excuse myself."

He smiled down at her. "Why?"

"Don't play coy. I am going to squirt all over the place if I don't take care of this."

"Ah, yes, management has made a request." He leaned in and told her what he wanted her to create.

She shivered and looked around. "Seriously?"

He chuckled. "Seriously."

"Where . . . oh. They brought the kit." Zera had her pack

near the throne; a small table with shot glasses was handy.

He picked her up and carried her to the throne, sitting down before tucking her on the arm of the chair. He took one of the flat pumps with the capture chamber, and he eased the fabric covering her out of the way. A light nuzzle and some strokes with his lips, and she started leaking. He attached the pump, and it hummed as he held it in his palm. He kept his hand on her until she had produced eight ounces. He turned the pump off and set it aside.

She tried to stop him from sucking, but she gasped. When he exposed her other breast and said, "Ah, kitten," she was embarrassed at how readily her body let down the milk for him.

He slid a hand under her skirt and stroked the slick petals of her sex carefully as he drank.

She didn't look at the crowd, didn't watch Zera prepping the tiny shots, she just looked at Salat's solid black eyes, and she held him to her as she shuddered in his arms.


Zera shared out the milk, and she grinned to the escorts. They had all been briefed on this. If they wanted to try, they could.

Putting pliant arousal and confidence into a shot wasn't something most beings could do, but Khytten managed it without any trouble.

Fifteen took a shot, shivered, and went to speak with a patron she had been flirting with. He was on her safe list, but they had never met. Apparently, that was about to change.

She felt hands on her waist. Tycho murmured in her ear. "Are you going to take a shot?"

"When the other escorts have taken one."

"You poured thirty; there are only fifteen escorts here. What are the others for?"

"Anyone who wants them."

He wandered over and took a shot for her and one for him. They did the shot, and there was a moment of shivering, and the warm hum of arousal ran through her. She turned to Tycho and kissed him, guiding him to a portion of the floor covered with cushions.

It was the start of a forty-person orgy, which Khytten and Salat had begun on the dais. Salat pulled his kitten into his lap, and they joined together, rising and falling, Khytten's eyes nearly closed, and her lips parted with every move. They linked and withdrew, and there were a lot of jealous gazes directed at Salat. Tough, it just went to show them that they needed to keep an open mind about the escorts. If they put their own preconceptions of what the escorts' bodies were supposed to do, they might find something spectacular.

Salat had gone for the basics and stayed for the extraordinary.

Susa was off with one of her favourite clients before the events of the last few weeks and renewing her acquaintance with her own body.

"Zera, you are a million miles away." Tycho nipped at her breast.

She inhaled sharply. "Sorry, dearest, just thinking in a few dimensions." She caressed his hair. "I am back now. All yours."

He laughed. "I truly doubt that, but we have you at night, and that's what matters."

Ryma came toward them, and she started suckling at Zera's breasts as Tycho slid into her. They were rocking together with hands and tongues moving in concert. They had all cum at least twice before Torun approached and lifted them, sliding his cock into her rear passage.

She blinked, and her eyes went wide. "What did you coat yourself with?"

"I asked Khytten for something specific, and based on the way you are quivering around me, it seems to be working." He laughed, and she saw Tycho's eyes were closed and his neck flexed. The effect was running through her.

He started moving, and she swallowed and asked with a strangled tone, "What did you ask for?"

"I asked for excitement and pleasure. It seems she gave me what I needed."

She leaned back into his slow slides. "She always does."

Tycho thrust deep into her, Ryma got the benefit of her left hand, and they rocked and moved together until they shook and clung together as one.

Zera looked over at the dais where Salat was stroking the hair back from Khytten's face. Khytten had one of the most adept skills for talking dirty that Zera had ever heard, but it was only with Salat that she had been given the opportunity to use it. He had given her the chance to use a lot of things, and he would help her keep evolving.

For now, Zera was in a tangle of some of the other people she loved best in the universe, so she could wait on figuring the next escort who could find the right active to make them happy.

If Zera's people had planted the genome change, Zera was going to defy their plans. She would build businesses, put actives under her thrall, and push the global society toward a better future by controlling their heroes, whether they wanted it or not.

# Author's Note

So . . . this took a turn. (I say that a lot.) It started out as a simple story, and then, it evolved into something that I had a lot of fun with.

Inspired by recent television programs, I posited that the thing most heroes would have trouble with is a sex life. Someone that they couldn't split in half during intimate moments, or a partner that couldn't be electrified, brainwashed, or other things of that nature.

It was a fun premise, and so, the Blind Date Corporation came about because those putting themselves forward for this purpose were entitled to their own privacy and secret identity. Baristas have the right to not be outed as a dominatrix with a sonic pulse for a pulse, right?

I look forward to playing in this world for a while. I find it very soothing.

Thanks for reading,

Viola Grace

# About the Author

Viola Grace (aka Zenina Masters) is a Canadian sci-fi/paranormal romance writer with ambitions to keep writing for the rest of her life. She specializes in short stories because the thrill of discovery, of all those firsts, is what keeps her writing.

An artist who enjoys a story that catches you up, whirls you around, and sets you down with a smile on your face is all she endeavours to be. She prefers to leave the drama to those who are better suited to it, she always goes for the cheap laugh.

In real life, she is now engaged in beekeeping, and her adventures can be found on the YouTube channel, Mystery Bees Apiary. Just look for the cartoon kittens.